"I feel like a teenager who's about to be caught necking,"

Nathan whispered, chuckling softly as he helped Gwen straighten her blouse.

Gwen just smiled. He actually looked discomfited, and she thought that was too alluring for words.

At that moment she felt something happen inside her. A funny, heated hitch in her heart. Gwen had never been in love before. She'd never experienced the feeling of falling for a man. Of feeling as if she wouldn't mind spending the rest of the night with him…or maybe even the rest of her life with him. But if she had to hazard a guess…she'd have to say that the emotion humming through her was just that.

Love.

Dear Reader,

What makes readers love Silhouette Romance? Fans who have sent mail and participated on our www.eHarlequin.com community bulletin boards say they enjoy the heart-thumping emotion, the noble strength of the heroines, the truly heroic nature of the men—all in a quick yet satisfying read. I couldn't have said it better!

This month we have some fantastic series for you. Bestselling author Lindsay McKenna visits use with *The Will To Love* (SR 1618), the latest in her thrilling cross-line adventure MORGAN'S MERCENARIES: ULTIMATE RESCUE. Jodi O'Donnell treats us with her BRIDGEWATER BACHELORS title, *The Rancher's Promise* (SR 1619), about sworn family enemies who fight the dangerous attraction sizzling between them.

You must pick up *For the Taking* (SR 1620) by Lilian Darcy. In this A TALE OF THE SEA, the last of the lost royal siblings comes home. And if that isn't dramatic enough, in Valerie Parv's *Crowns and a Cradle* (SR 1621), part of THE CARRAMER LEGACY, a struggling single mom discovers she's a princess!

Finishing off the month are Myrna Mackenzie's *The Billionaire's Bargain* (SR 1622)—the second book in the latest WEDDING AUCTION series—about a most tempting purchase. And *The Sheriff's 6-Year-Old Secret* (SR 1623) is Donna Clayton's tearjerker.

I hope you enjoy this month's selection. Be sure to drop us a line or visit our Web site to let us know what we're doing right—and any particular favorite topics you want to revisit. Happy reading!

Mary-Theresa Hussey

Mary-Theresa Hussey
Senior Editor

Please address questions and book requests to:
Silhouette Reader Service
U.S.: 3010 Walden Ave., P.O. Box 1325, Buffalo, NY 14269
Canadian: P.O. Box 609, Fort Erie, Ont. L2A 5X3

The Sheriff's 6-Year-Old Secret

Donna Clayton

SILHOUETTE *Romance*®

Published by Silhouette Books

America's Publisher of Contemporary Romance

To the Delaware Moms

Thank you for your friendship and support

SILHOUETTE BOOKS

ISBN 0-373-19623-7

THE SHERIFF'S 6-YEAR-OLD SECRET

Copyright © 2002 by Donna Fasano

This edition published by arrangement with Harlequin Books S.A.

Visit Silhouette at www.eHarlequin.com

Printed in U.S.A.

DONNA CLAYTON

is the recipient of the Diamond Author Award for Literary Achievement 2000, as well as two Holt Medallions. She became a writer through her love of reading. As a child, she marveled at her ability to travel the world, experience swashbuckling adventures and meet amazingly bold and daring people without ever leaving the shade of the huge oak in her very own backyard. She takes great pride in knowing that, through her work, she provides her readers the chance to indulge in some purely selfish romantic entertainment.

One of her favorite pastimes is traveling. Her other interests include walking, reading, visiting with friends, teaching Sunday school, cooking and baking, and she still collects cookbooks, too. In fact, her house is overrun with them.

Please write to Donna care of Silhouette Books. She'd love to hear from you!

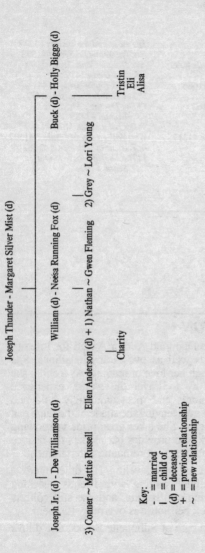

Joseph Thunder - Margaret Silver Mist (d)

Joseph Jr. (d) - Dee Williamson (d)   William (d) - Neesa Running Fox (d)   Buck (d) - Holly Biggs (d)

3) Conner ~ Mattie Russell   Ellen Anderson (d) + 1) Nathan ~ Gwen Fleming   2) Grey ~ Lori Young

Charity

Tristin
Eli
Alisa

Key:
- = married
| = child of
(d) = deceased
+ = previous relationship
~ = new relationship

Joseph Thunder is a well-respected shaman of his Kolheek people. But he is a sad man. No one should outlive his child; however, he has outlived all three of his sons and daughters-in-law. He has raised his five grandsons—his granddaughter was taken away from the reservation by her mother——and he's determined to see that his grandchildren live happy and successful lives...

1) Nathan's story: THE SHERIFF'S 6-YEAR-OLD SECRET (RS#1623)
2) Grey's story: THE DOCTOR'S PREGNANT PROPOSAL (RS#1635)
3) Conner's story: THUNDER IN THE NIGHT (RS#1647)

Chapter One

The last thing Nathan Thunder needed was more trouble.

"Looks like more trouble is just what you're in for, though." His murmur held a distinct quality of resigned despair as he dropped the phone receiver into its cradle. He scrubbed at the back of his neck and then let his fingers worry back and forth across his jaw.

Having just stepped into the job of sheriff of Smoke Valley Reservation a few short weeks ago, he was doing all he could to unite his small staff into a team. He'd returned to the reservation after a long absence and now needed to spend loads of time allowing the residents to get to know him again. A law officer who didn't have the respect and trust of the community couldn't carry out his duties effectively.

Not that Nathan was an outsider, by any means.

Yes, he'd left Smoke Valley more than ten years ago to attend the New York City Police Academy. He'd joined the NYPD and was proud of his distinguished career. But he'd been back to visit his friends and family on the rez many times. And he was back for good now. If truth be known, he was happy about the move, as well as relieved; this job seemed to have put his haunting fear to rest.

Oh, he was confident he could do a good job as sheriff—he'd unify his officers and garner the community's trust. He was certain of it. He only wished that confidence extended itself to his personal life. Now *that* was where the real trouble lay: in his personal life. Namely, his daughter, Charity.

His daughter. He still couldn't get over the astounding turn of events that had brought this child into his life just five short weeks ago.

When Nathan thought of little girls, he imagined sugar and spice and everything nice. Sweet smiles. Frilly dresses. Ballet lessons. Butterfly kisses. Now the Great Spirit above knew Nathan had no understanding whatsoever of children, but six-year-old Charity seemed to break every single label ever slapped on the female of the species. She had a rough-and-tumble attitude, an aversion to any clothing with even a hint of a ruffle and a speak-your-mind tongue that often had him at a loss for words.

Her wildness needed taming. And the short phone conversation he'd just had with the principal of the local elementary school only cemented the notion into his brain. It seemed his bruiser of a daughter had socked a fellow student during recess. On her first day in the first-grade class, no less.

He whistled, shaking his head. ''What a way to make a first impression.''

After alerting the dispatcher of his plans, Nathan got into his car and drove the short distance to the school. He parked, cut the ignition and walked up the sidewalk. The closer he got to the doors, the more his feeling of doom increased. The heels of his shoes echoed in the wide, empty corridor as he searched for the first-grade classroom. Butterflies began to dance a jig in his stomach. Then suddenly he nearly chuckled out loud at himself. It was quite comical that he could calmly face down a fugitive with a deadly weapon, yet the idea of meeting with Charity's teacher had him feeling tense and jittery.

The woman was turned away from him when he entered the classroom, but one look at the mass of flaming curls tumbling down her back, one glimpse of the lissome, curvy figure told him he'd already met Charity's teacher.

In the line of duty.

Just as Gwen set the chalkboard eraser on the metal ledge, her skin tingled with the ingrained awareness that alerted her to someone's presence behind her. She took a deep, steeling breath. The principal had set up this parent-teacher meeting for her. Not having spoken to Charity's father herself, Gwen had no idea if the man would be rational and unruffled...or if she'd be facing a Brahma bull. As a teacher, she'd learned to expect the unexpected when it came to dealing with parents. All she'd been told was that he was coming.

Fixing a reassuring smile on her mouth, she turned. However, the sight of the police officer standing at the threshold of her classroom made her stomach turn queasy.

While growing up, she'd had quite a few experiences where the police showed up at her house. Each and every encounter had been frightening.

Her countenance fell and she had trouble drawing a breath.

His shoulders massive, the man seemed to fill the doorway. His face, with its classic Native American features, was handsome beyond belief and caused heat to curl inside her, but at the same time the implications of that olive-and-gray uniform, of that shiny metal badge on his chest, made her go cold all over. Like steam and ice—it was the oddest sensation she'd ever experienced.

The scariest thing about this moment, she realized, was that she recognized this man as the law officer who had lectured her brother soundly for shoplifting a candy bar just last week. It was strange that she'd been bombarded with the same hot-cold feeling then as she was now.

Thank heavens she'd been there in the store when the incident had occurred. She'd been in such a rush to pay for the candy her brother had slipped into his pocket that she'd spilled the entire contents of her purse on the wide wooden countertop. Keys, change, pictures, a tube of lipstick had all gone astray, bouncing and tumbling out of reach.

The fact that Brian had done such a thing had been bad enough. But when the policeman arrived, she'd gone all shaky inside. She'd never been so embarrassed in her life. She'd been truly grateful that the store owner hadn't pressed charges. And she'd been just as thankful that the officer had taken Brian aside and given him a good talking-to about the trouble he could get into by taking things that didn't belong to him.

If the officer was showing up at her place of work, Brian must have done something horrendous. Her knees went wobbly as warm rubber.

"What's he done now?" Trepidation made her voice raspy, and she barely made it to her chair in one piece. It felt as if all her joints had turned to rusty hinges from which the pins had been pulled. She was so glad the chair was already pulled out as she sank into it. "It must be bad if you're coming to find me at school."

Last week she'd been startled by how handsome the Kolheek officer was. His eyes were a deep, rich brown, his hair as black and shiny as a crow's wing glinting in the sunshine. Parted in the middle, his hair feathered back away from his face, long enough that only the lobes of his ears were visible. His high, sharp cheekbones gave him a noble air. The sharp angle of his jaw had become even sharper, had taken on an extreme seriousness, and his dark eyes had intensified with a stern and steady stare as he'd chastised her brother outside the store.

Now, she saw, his face was just as gorgeous, his hair just as silky, but his mahogany gaze was soft with compassion.

"Hold on a second."

His tone had gone just as gentle as his expression and he lifted his hand, palm outward, to her.

"I'm not here on business."

Then his brow puckered and he became obviously flustered.

"Well...I am here on business but...what I mean is..."

Mild frustration made his expression rather comical, and if Gwen hadn't been so upset by the sight of him, intimidated by his presence and that uniform, she'd have smiled. But the present situation with her brother was too overwhelming for her to see any humor in having a police officer show up at her place of employment.

She was so scared for her brother that she found herself unable to speak.

"I'm not here on *police* business," he rushed to add.

Gwen felt her lips form a silent "Oh," and she nodded. She let out her breath, not realizing before this moment that she'd been holding it.

"So if you're not here about Brian, Officer—" her voice was still raspy "—I'm afraid I'm confused. What can I do for you?" Glancing at her wristwatch, she said, "I don't have much time to give you right now. You see, I'm expecting a parent—"

"I'm the expectant parent."

He shook his head when he realized what he'd said. Tipping up his chin, he tried again, "I'm the expecting parent." The sigh he heaved was filled to the brim with aggravation. "I'm the parent you're expecting."

The relief that flooded through her was dizzying. She wanted to let out a sigh, so happy was she to discover that he wasn't there about Brian. However, in the same instant, she was acutely cognizant of how flustered he was. It seemed as though he was as thrown off by their sudden reacquaintance as she.

He chuckled, one shoulder lifting in a shrug. "I'm not a complete and utter idiot, I assure you. And I do have a full working knowledge of the English language. I'm just a little nervous about…" He let the rest of his sentence fade.

She realized then that it wasn't seeing her again that had him in such a tizzy, it was the occasion. This was probably his first parent-teacher meeting.

"You're Charity Thunder's father." It was more a statement than a question, but she wanted him to know she *finally* was clear about who he was and what he was doing here.

Now that the situation had become a little less tangled, she felt it was her obligation to gather her wits about her and put on a professional face. However, the blatant fact that he was the cop who had chewed out her brother for breaking the law was enough to instill a hefty amount of awkwardness in her.

"Yes." He seemed relieved to have his identity straightened out. "And I want you to know right off I don't condone hitting. I apologize for Charity's behavior." He looked around the classroom. "Where is she, by the way? I thought she'd be here. I'm more than happy to show her that you and I are a united front against this kind of behavior."

Gwen felt herself relax. She was pleased to realize this was one parent she wasn't going to have to argue with about a student's conduct. So often parents were unwilling to recognize or admit when their children were in the wrong.

"Charity's with Principal Halley," she told him. "I thought, since we didn't get a chance to meet before school started, that today would be a good time for us to sit and chat."

He nodded. "Well, just so you know, my daughter's going to get an earful from me on the subject of hitting her fellow students."

"Oh, now," she said softly, "I think Charity realizes that she made a mistake."

Sunlight streamed through the window, glinting off his badge. She thought it ironic that just last week this man had had to reprimand her brother and today she'd corrected his daughter. The idea made her a little uncomfortable, as if she and this stranger had too much of a hand in each other's personal lives.

But that's silly, she thought. After all, they were only doing their jobs.

However, something akin to intuition—no, something more astute than mere intuition, something soul-deep—told her this meeting, *this man,* would mean something significant to her.

Oh, come on now, girl, she silently chastised. *You've been spending too much time reading about Kolheek mysticism.*

After a couple of seconds that seemed positively charged with the uneasiness that pulsed through her, she motioned to him with a wave of her hand. "Come on in and have a seat. Let's talk."

The only chairs available, other than her own, were built especially for pint-size, six-year-old bodies. He straddled one of the small seats and attempted to lower himself into it. He was a big man, and the honed bulk of him made the chair seem even smaller than it already was.

"I'm sorry about the seating," she said, automatically rising and coming around her desk. "But this is all I have to offer."

"It's fine."

But it was obvious to her that, with his knees bent up around his shoulders, he was surely in a most uncomfortable position. The situation was not fine and he was too polite to say so.

"How about if we just sit on the desks?" she offered.

His handsome face took on a look of incredible gratitude at the suggestion. She slid onto the top of the wooden desk that was closest to her. The officer— she still couldn't get over how unsettled she was by that uniform—straightened his contorted posture and sat down on a neighboring desktop.

"Better?" she asked.

"Much."

She forced herself to smile. "Good. Now that I know who you are, let me introduce myself." She reached her hand out to him, and when he took it, the heat of him shocked her, short-circuited her thoughts, and for a second she couldn't remember her own name.

"Gwen." The word finally burst from her tongue. "Gwen Fleming." She pumped his hand, drawing in a huge gulp of air, hoping to calm the astonishing riot going on inside her. "I'm Charity's teacher."

"And I'm her father, Nathan Thunder," he provided.

He pressed his free hand against the back of hers, enveloping her in a blanket of feverish warmth.

"It's good to meet you." His mouth widened with sincerity.

Gwen felt hot. Cold. Panicked. If she didn't sever contact with him soon, perspiration would surely break out across her brow. What in heaven's name had gotten into her?

He released her hand, leaned back a bit and hitched his left ankle over his right knee. His fingers curled nonchalantly around his shin and Gwen couldn't help but notice the tapered length of them. She wondered how they'd feel caressing her cheek.

She stifled her gasping reaction to the totally shocking thought. Her eyes widened. Something was really wrong here. A notion as strange as that one shouldn't be in her head. This man was the parent of one of her students.

"I know that Charity missed—"

Her gaze seemed to take on a life all its own as it settled on his lips. She became mesmerized by the way his sexy mouth formed words.

"—the first few days of school—"

The bow centering his top lip with its two perfect points was so…attractive. How would it feel to gently drag her tongue across its surface? What would his mouth taste like against her own?

"—what with the testing Principal Halley insisted on."

Gwen blinked. *Dragging her tongue across his lip? Tasting his mouth?* Had she totally lost her mind? Then other questions rolled through her head. Missed days? Testing? Oh, Lord. What in the world had he been talking about?

"I do understand the need for the tests, though," Nathan Thunder continued.

The man obviously hadn't realized that Gwen's sexual fantasies had made her temporarily check out of their conversation, and for that she was mightily grateful.

"As the principal explained," he said, "since Charity didn't attend kindergarten last year, it was necessary to see where she is, knowledge-wise, compared to the other students."

He smiled again, and even though she knew perfectly well autumn had arrived, Gwen felt as if she'd been struck full in the face with the heat of the midsummer sun. She pressed her lips together and did her best to focus on the topic at hand.

Charity's father continued, ''I will admit that I'm happy she was placed with her peers, rather than put back with the five-year-olds.''

Gwen scrambled around in her thought processes until she was up to speed in this conversation. ''W-well, Mr. Thunder, the tests showed your daughter met all the first-grade requirements,'' she said.

''Nathan,'' he said. ''Please call me Nathan.''

Her smile was automatic. But her insides were nothing but chaos. ''Only if you'll call me Gwen.''

A look passed across his mahogany gaze, an unreadable expression that caused her spine to prickle with a needle-sharp sensation that had her feeling the need to arch her back like a cat. Her reaction to this man was terribly unprofessional. She'd better be careful.

''Even without the kindergarten experience—'' she forced herself to ignore her physical reaction to him, to remain attentive to the discussion at hand ''—Charity is on par with the average students in the class.''

His head bobbed slowly up and down. ''I brought all this up because I'm wondering if the days she missed might have contributed to this, um…hitting incident. It seems to me that children form bonds very quickly. And with Charity not being here with the others for the first days of classes…''

''You're right. Kids do connect almost instantly. They develop friendships, fashion allegiances, form hierarchies, no matter how hard we try to dissuade such behavior. However, they're also very fickle creatures, switching alliances frequently.'' Her mouth pulled wide with a grin. ''I want you to know that— other than the recess incident—she did very well today at getting along with her classmates.''

''Well, is the little boy okay?'' he asked. ''The one she fought with?''

''He's fine. I spoke with his mother when she picked him up from school just a bit ago. I explained everything.''

He looked so miserable that his daughter might have hurt a fellow student that Gwen's heart went out to him. She felt it would help him immensely if she let him in on a big secret. ''Truly, Mr. Thunder—''

''Nathan,'' he reminded her.

''Nathan,'' she repeated, ''I have a sneaking suspicion that something good just might come out of all this.''

Apparent bewilderment made him frown. She glanced toward the door to make sure no one could overhear what she was about to reveal.

''You see, even after only a few days of school, Billy Whitefeather has shown a…well, a propensity toward bullying the other children. By defending herself, Charity has shown the rest of the class that they don't have to be fearful of him.''

This information seemed to help smooth his brow a bit, and again, Gwen was acutely aware of how handsome the man was.

''But I did have to stress with Charity that hitting won't be tolerated,'' she went on, forcing herself to ignore the pleasant warmth the man caused to radiate throughout her entire body. "With what's happening all over this country…there's so much violence in our schools these days…and kids aren't feeling safe…well, we've adopted a no-tolerance policy. And even though ninety-nine point nine percent of aggression won't lead to anything more than name-calling and an occasional shove, we still have to take action. We still have to let the children know that violent behavior—in any form—is wrong. Charity seems to understand that."

"Of course," he told her. "And I agree whole-heartedly. You can rest assured that I'll reiterate that with her on the way home."

"And I want you to know," Gwen continued, "I had a long discussion with Billy. I tried to make him understand that his actions and his words only aggravated the problem."

Instigated them, really, she wanted to say. But she didn't. As a teacher and responsible adult, she had to represent every single one of her students in the fairest way possible.

"Well, if I know Charity—" Nathan's expression turned sheepish, and Gwen thought it terribly charming "—she probably gave Billy a few choice words of her own." Amazement made his brows raise a fraction and he shook his head. "In the few weeks since this child entered my life, she's proved to have a sharp tongue."

"She does speak her mind, doesn't she?" Gwen chuckled and suddenly remembered an encounter she'd had with the child. "In fact, she asked me first thing this morning if I forgot to brush my hair."

His eyes went round with dismay and his mouth dropped open. He blurted, "Y-your hair is beautiful."

Gwen knew he was only trying to make up for his daughter's infraction, but the compliment had her blushing with pure pleasure even so.

Reaching out, she touched his sleeve reassuringly. "Don't worry. I wasn't insulted. My students often comment about my unruly hair. I just explain that it's hard to keep curls like mine under control."

Suddenly she felt the need to reverse gears a step or two.

"If you don't mind my asking—" absently she laced her fingers together and placed them in her lap "—what did you mean just now when you said in the few weeks since Charity entered your life?"

One of his muscular shoulders lifted in a shrug. "At the beginning of last month...I wasn't even aware of Charity's existence. You see, Charity's mother and I dated for a while. A very short while. We broke up years ago and I never heard from the woman again. Until she had me contacted last month."

"Had you contacted?" Gwen couldn't hide her confusion. "I don't understand."

"She couldn't call herself. Ellen was ill. Extremely ill." His jaw tensed. "She was dying, actually. And she needed me to take Charity."

"Oh, my," Gwen breathed. "You must have been...surprised to learn you're a father. Incredulous,

really. Saddened by the woman's illness, of course.''
It was an amazing story. She couldn't imagine all that
he must have experienced while learning what was
sure to have been life-altering news.

He heaved a sigh. ''I felt all those things and more.
I was forced to deal with some big changes in my
life. Ellen's illness. Her funeral. And at the same time
I was attempting to cultivate some kind of relationship with this little girl. Do you have any idea how
difficult it is to explain to a child that her mother is
going away? *Forever?* I'm still not sure Charity un-
derstands.''

Her heart pinching with compassion, Gwen
couldn't help but remember when her own mother
died and she'd been the one who had had to explain
things to her brother, so she really did understand.

''It must have been awful,'' she murmured. ''For
both of you, I'm sure.''

''I wanted to get Charity out of the city—''

He blinked and his tongue smoothed across his
dusky lips. A strange tingling sensation rushed across
every inch of Gwen's skin. She stifled the shiver that
threatened to rock through her.

''—so I brought her here to Smoke Valley.''

The way his dark gaze slid from hers, she couldn't
help but think there was much more to his reasons
for leaving New York City than he was willing to
reveal to her, a total stranger.

''I was quitting one job, finding another. Packing
up my apartment, cleaning out Ellen's. Searching for
a place here on the rez for me and Charity to live.

Dealing with problems at the new job. You'd be amazed how hard it is for people to get used to a new boss." He shook his head. "Poor Charity must feel as if she's been tossed into a barrel with someone she's only known a short while and sent rolling and crashing down a rocky mountainside."

Gwen could easily imagine the feeling. Amazingly, that description matched what she was experiencing simply sitting here talking with the man.

"I didn't know that all this was going on in Charity's life," she said. "I'm glad you told me. I'll be extra patient with her. And I'll look for any overt signs of stress in her behavior."

His chin snapped up. "You think that's why she fought with that little boy today? Because she's stressed because of all the changes taking place in her life?"

Gwen shook her head emphatically. "No, I don't think that at all. I'm certain she was simply reacting to some mean-spirited comments made by one of her classmates, that's all. I would tell you if I thought there was more to it, honestly I would. Charity was just standing up for herself. And as I've already told you, I think she showed the class today that Billy's bullying doesn't have to be tolerated. The children have other outlets. They have me. They can come to me. And I've told them so."

After a moment he gave his head a slow, grim shake. "I guess you can tell I don't have a clue about raising a daughter. I have no experience at this at all. I'm a single guy whose only responsibility up until a few weeks ago was showing up for work every day and paying my rent on time.''

"Oh, now," she crooned softly. His self-doubt stirred her empathy something fierce. "Give yourself more credit than that."

She felt such an overwhelming urge to encourage and support this man. Gwen tried to imagine what it would be like to wake up one morning and discover that not only do you have a daughter but that you're now going to be her sole guardian. The idea was mind-boggling. The poor guy must have reeled when he found out about Charity. Heck, from the sound it, he was *still* reeling.

"All you need to do is love her," Gwen told him. "That's the number-one key to raising a healthy child. Unconditional love." Then she smiled. "That, and firm discipline."

He seemed surprised by this last suggestion.

The silent questions in his dark gaze had her elaborating, "I've only been working with youngsters for a few years, but the one thing I've learned is that kids love to shove at the boundaries that have been set for them." Her eyes twinkled with the merriment she felt. "As adults, it's our job to shove them right back. Metaphorically speaking, of course."

He laughed, and Gwen was amazed by how much she liked the rich sound. She'd have loved to press her palm to his chest and feel the vibration of it.

The idea made her eyes widen a fraction. It was clear to her that, despite the disquieting, memory-stirring uniform he wore, Nathan Thunder was having the most startling effect on her.

"Love and discipline. I'll try to remember that."

She squeezed his forearm. "You'll do just fine. You'll see."

His gorgeous eyes clouded with skepticism, but he made no further comment. Finally he said, "Thank you, Gwen, for being so reasonable about the mess Charity got herself into today."

A soft chuckle escaped her throat. "When you choose to work with kids, your middle name had better be 'reasonable' or you aren't going to survive for very long." All this talk of being levelheaded with children triggered the memory of what had happened last week with her brother.

"I owe you a hefty dose of appreciation, as well," she said, her tone growing serious. "You, too, were very reasonable last week with my brother. I thank you for taking the time to talk to him."

"That was all part of my job. I'd much rather give a kid a good lecture meant to scare the bejesus out of him than see him get himself into some real trouble later in life."

Gwen hoped that Brian's run-in with the law would have him walking the straight and narrow path. But for some reason, she feared that wasn't the case. There was simply too much secrecy about where he was and whom he spent his time with these days. Some of that, she was certain, was just part of being a teenager. But Brian was harboring a great deal of anger and resentment, and Gwen felt her brother had no intention of venting those negative feelings in positive ways.

"How is he?" Nathan asked. "Your brother— Brian's his name, isn't it?"

"Brian, yes." Inadvertently she sighed. "He's... okay."

Obviously sensing her hesitance, he coaxed, "Is everything really all right at home? Are your parents very upset with Brian for what happened at the store?"

"N-no. Well...," she stammered, "you see, it's just me and Brian."

It was clear that this revelation surprised him. He tried to temper his reaction, but this news caused questions to form in his head. Gwen could plainly see that. However, before he could speak, movement at the classroom doorway plucked at their attention.

"Dad."

Gwen smiled and invited Charity into the room with a wave of her hand. The child looked so innocent with her mop of dark curls and her milky complexion. At first glance, no one would have guessed that this little girl was capable of knocking a fellow student on his behind. Gwen stifled the grin that threatened to break out across her face.

"Mrs. Halley told me to come down here. She had to leave to pick up her son at day care."

Glancing at the clock, Gwen said, "I should let you go, too. I'm sure you have a busy evening planned. And I still have some things to do to get ready for class tomorrow, then I have to get home. I don't like to leave Brian alone for too long.''

''Miss Fleming?''

''Yes, Charity?'' Gwen directed her full attention to the child.

''Am I allowed to come to school tomorrow? I promise not to hit Billy again.'' Then the girl shook her head, her face taking on a clear and unmistakable expression of long suffering. ''No matter how much he might need it.''

The opinion was delivered without a trace of guile; however, Nathan went pale at his daughter's unexpected aside. The best Gwen could do was bite back the laughter that nearly got the best of her.

''Of course you can come back to school,'' she said. She bent down so that she was face-to-face with Charity. ''And if Billy does or says something to upset you, you come see me, okay? Just like we talked about today.''

Charity nodded. ''I will.''

Gwen straightened and, smiling, reached out her hand to Nathan. She hoped she could silently convey to the man that his daughter's comment wasn't anything out of the norm. She heard those kinds of outlandish judgments on a daily basis from her six-year-old students. However, now just wasn't a good time to tell him, not with Charity within earshot.

''It was good to meet you, Nathan.''

''Same here,'' he said.

His apologetic look seemed to soften, and she got the distinct impression that he'd somehow understood the silent message she'd attempted to send. His dark eyes softened. ''Thanks for everything.''

Her smile broadened. ''You're very welcome.''

He and Charity turned to go, and the oddest sensation washed through Gwen's body. As she watched father and daughter walk out of the classroom, she couldn't get over the feeling that her life would never quite be the same.

Chapter Two

Her hand felt so small and vulnerable in his as the two of them walked across the school parking lot toward his car. Even after weeks of having this child in his life, he still felt overwhelmed at times by this circumstance he found himself in.

This new stage in his life—being a parent—certainly was taking some getting used to. Every single aspect of it. He was oblivious to the beautiful blue sky as memories bombarded him. Early on, he and Charity had had a long conversation regarding what she should call him, and it had been such a poignant moment Nathan knew he'd never forget it for as long as he lived.

"So what do I call you?" she'd asked matter-of-factly less then twenty-four hours after their first meeting.

Nathan had been taken aback by the blunt question. "Well, what would you like to call me?"

"I've had a Daddy-Chuck and a Daddy-Steve. I've had a Daddy-Toby and a Daddy-Tony." Her face had scrunched up. "I used to get 'em mixed up and Mommy would get mad at me. But it was hard to remember, ya know?"

"I understand." But he hadn't really. What had Ellen been thinking, bringing so many men into Charity's life? But then, he hadn't really been with the woman long enough to get to know who Ellen was or what she wanted out of life. He had no idea what kind of childhood she'd had or what kind of baggage she'd carried from her past, so he really had no business judging her lifestyle.

"I don't wanna call you Daddy-anything."

"You don't?" Nathan's throat constricted at the sudden forlorn look that clouded his daughter's eyes.

Finally she whispered, "Daddies don't stay."

"Oh, honey," he'd crooned, soft and assuring, "I'm not going anywhere. I mean that. You're going to be with me forever."

Her little head had tilted to one side and she'd nonchalantly replied, "We'll see."

His eyes had burned with emotion. He'd been able to tell that she desperately wanted his promise to go unbroken, but her trust was obviously something she didn't give away easily. Not after all she'd evidently been through in her young life. Only time would prove to her that Nathan meant what he said.

"You could call me just plain Nathan," he suggested.

Her brow puckered. "Just Plain Nathan sounds kinda funny."

"No." He'd chuckled. "I mean, Nathan. You could call me Nathan."

She made no comment at first, but he could tell her thoughts were churning. Then her chin had thrust out boldly, her eyes avoiding his, as she blurted, "But every kid needs a dad, don'tcha think? I could call you Dad, couldn't I?"

His heart had swelled painfully. "Sure you could. That would be just fine."

Yes, that had been one exchange that had given him great insight. Charity, even at such a young age, was striving to achieve some sort of normalcy for herself amidst the chaos of the world around her.

Now he helped her into the back seat, shut the door and then slid behind the wheel. He listened a moment as she struggled to latch her seat belt, quelling the urge to offer her help. He'd discovered she was an independent little thing, and if he offered to come to her aid too quickly, she'd become exasperated with him.

Casting a glance at her in the rearview mirror, he smiled. She was the image of her mother, with her head of tight, dark curls and her skin like porcelain. So small and innocent. However, today's events had to be talked about, no matter how much he'd like to bypass the moment.

After he heard the latch click securely, he asked, "You want to tell me what happened today?"

Her gaze met his in the mirror. "I know I'm in trouble for hitting Billy Whitefeather. But he said Charity was a stupid name. He said I wasn't Indian. And that I didn't belong in this school."

Nathan's nod was nearly imperceptible. He had suspected Charity wouldn't have lashed out without being provoked.

"So," she continued in a rush, "I told him White-feather was the stupidest name in the whole, wide universe. And that my dad was sheriff. And that I could go to this school if I wanted to."

So he'd been correct when he'd told Charity's teacher that his daughter could give as good as she got. A smile threatened the firm line of his mouth, but he wrestled it into submission. Now wasn't the time to laugh at his daughter's antics. He needed to nip this behavior in the bud.

"He made a fist and I knew he was gonna hit me," she explained. "I was scared, but I slugged him first. And ya know something?" Unadulterated wonder made her eyes go round. "He cried like a big, fat baby."

Nathan knew it was wrong, but he'd be lying if he didn't plainly identify the emotion flashing though him as nothing less than pride. Even though he was brand-new at this dad business, he guessed that no parent wanted their child to be a pushover. He was happy to discover that Charity could stand up for herself. But it was certain that they'd have to work on the means she used to do so.

"It's not nice to hit people," he told her.

"But Billy said—"

"I heard you the first time. But you need to know, Charity, you can't go around hitting everyone who says something you don't like."

"But—"

"Honey—" his tone was firm "—there are no buts. Hitting is wrong."

The look on her face told him she was crushed. All Nathan wanted to do was give her a big hug and assure her that everything was going to be okay. But he forced himself to remain silent. She needed to contemplate her behavior. To realize the magnitude of her actions.

Our job is to shove them right back. Gwen's advice regarding setting firm boundaries floated through his mind.

Nathan's fingers were trembling as he placed the key in the ignition and fired up the engine. He sighed. Being the disciplinarian was a necessary part of parenting, Charity's teacher had just informed him, but it wasn't a part of his new job as dad that he was going to enjoy very much.

The morning sun glowed through the windowpanes, rays of light glinting directly on the large jar of pennies that sat on the battered credenza. The jar was significant to Nathan. While working with the NYPD, he'd placed a penny in the jar every single day that he'd finished a shift and returned to the station house alive.

Lucky pennies. His jar of luck. It reminded him to be grateful for every day he was here on earth.

Several of his colleagues who had worked as cops in the city hadn't been so lucky. All Nathan had to do was close his eyes to visualize the grief-stricken, tearstained faces of the wives and children of his fallen comrades. Those funerals he'd attended had been the reason he'd remained single all these years. Those sad occasions had also been the reason he'd brought Charity here to Smoke Valley Reservation. To a slower, safer way of life.

Now, however, one particularly new penny in the jar caught the sunlight, gleaming like coppery fire. Immediately Gwen Fleming's glorious head of red hair came rushing into his mind with the force of a flash of lightning.

Wispy heat curled down low in his belly as a thundering bolt of pure desire rumbled through him. Nathan's jaw tightened. It had been three days since he'd met his daughter's teacher, and since then the woman had invaded his thoughts more times than he cared to admit. She was a looker, she was, with her head of wild ginger curls and a smile that could make a man give up his life's fortune if she asked for it.

The woman was a tactile person, someone who was comfortable touching those within range. She'd reached out to him several times during their meeting, and each and every time Nathan had felt the air heat up, felt his heart thud like the hooves of a racehorse, his blood rushing through his veins.

He'd been surprised when she'd said she and her brother were alone. He'd wanted to ask her more about her situation. But Charity's arrival had interrupted them.

Raising a teen was an awesome task. Nathan was impressed by Gwen's dedication and her willingness to take responsibility for her brother. He couldn't help but wonder how she'd come to find herself in such a situation. He'd have loved the chance to talk to Gwen about it further.

"Why don't you just admit it?" he whispered to himself.

You'd have done just about anything to make that meeting last just a little longer. You lusted after that fiery-haired woman right there in that first-grade classroom, amid all the bright primary-colored shapes and alphabet letters hanging on the walls, and you've been lusting after her ever since.

He sighed, resting his elbow on his desk and his jaw in the V between his thumb and fingers, blind to the forms on his desk needing completion.

It really hadn't mattered that he and Gwen had been in the most inopportune place, he realized. A classroom where children learned and played sure wasn't the perfect location for him to experience such gut-wrenching desire. Nonetheless, that was exactly where he had experienced it.

Getting involved in his daughter's teacher's private life should have been the last thing on his mind. He had papers to file, forms to complete, a police station to run. A little girl to raise.

Still, the sunlight continued to gleam through the window, making that jar of copper pennies wink and smile…reminding him of one beautiful and extraordinary woman.

Gwen paced the close confines of her small living room, anxiety nibbling at her nerves like ravenous mice after a slice of fresh Swiss. Where was Brian?

She'd arrived home from school to an empty house. No note. No phone message. Nothing.

He was often absent when she got in from work. But he always left her a note. Well, almost always. And he never failed to return before dinner.

But tonight the meat loaf she'd cooked sat on the counter, stone cold. The mashed potatoes had congealed into a hard lump. And there was simply no hope for the limp green beans stuck to the bottom of the pan.

The sky had darkened long ago, and Gwen didn't have any idea where her brother might be, or what trouble he might be getting himself into. Ever since that shoplifting incident, she'd been worried sick. She didn't know the names of any of the boys he'd met since their move to Smoke Valley. Brian had been steadily uncommunicative about his friends. She didn't have a clue whom to call or what to do. For all she knew, he could have been struck by a car while he was riding his bike and was lying unconscious in the emergency ward of the local hospital, in the neighboring town of Mountview. During *that* moment of panic, Gwen had called the dispatcher at the Smoke Valley police station. The woman had been so nice in her efforts to calm Gwen and had assured her that no accidents had been reported.

Still, the lesson plans Gwen had intended to organize for her students sat on the table, untouched. Worry had her too upset to think straight, too distressed to eat.

So she paced. Wrung her hands. And waited.

The knock on the front door nearly made her jump right out of her skin. She rushed to the door, sure that her brother must have lost his key.

The sight of Nathan Thunder standing on her doorstep stole every thought from her head.

"Evening, Gwen," he greeted her. "My dispatcher got word to me that you called. I thought I'd stop by and check on you. Is everything okay?"

The concern on his handsome face nearly made her knees buckle. All Gwen wanted to do was lean on him, unload all her troubles onto his shoulders. He was barely in the door when she let her concerns roll off her tongue.

"I don't know where Brian is. He's never been this late before. He could be out there getting into trouble. He could be hurt. He could be—"

"Okay, now—"

His voice was soft, gentle, and so were his hands as he slid his fingers over her upper arms. He pulled her against his chest.

"—don't let your imagination get the best of you, Gwen."

Something happened when he embraced her. The molecules in the air heated and swirled, danced and constricted. Gwen felt as if she'd suddenly been enveloped by a warm, downy blanket.

The smoky spice of his cologne filled her lungs like a drug. For some reason, the idea of laying her head on his shoulder didn't seem the least bit strange. He held her for what seemed a delicious eternity. She felt safe. She felt as if nothing bad could ever happen to her. Soon her heartbeat steadied and her tense muscles relaxed.

Leaning away from her, yet obviously unwilling to release her completely, he asked, "You feeling better?"

Although she felt impelled to answer him with a small nod, leaving the safe haven of his arms was the last thing she wanted to do. This hazy stupor held her a willing captive.

Then she began to tremble with some unnamable thing, something that had nothing whatsoever to do with fear and distress over her brother. A silent yet humming electricity seemed to crackle about them, snapping and sparkling like bare high-voltage wires.

How had this energy manifested itself so instantaneously? Or had it been there all along and she was only now comprehending it? And where, she wondered, was the vibrant current going to lead?

She studied his gaze as he studied hers. Of one

thing she was certain—wherever it led, her drowsy mind reasoned, she was eager to follow.

Brian pushed his way through the front door.

"Hey."

As he spoke the greeting, he lifted his chin at her and Nathan as if coming in this late was commonplace, as if he came home every day to find his sister in a man's arms.

Immediately Nathan released Gwen, and without his nearness to warm her, she was hit with the sensation of being chilled to the bone. But the appearance of her brother caused her to be bombarded with numerous emotions all at once: relief that he was safe and sound, anger that he'd caused her such worry, irritation that he seemed untroubled by this whole situation. Heck, he acted as if there wasn't a situation at all!

"Hey, man—" Brian grinned at Nathan "—I don't know what brought the police here, but whatever it was, I didn't do it."

"You're not in any trouble," Nathan assured her brother. "I'm just here to check on your sister." Solemnity knitted his brow. "She was worried about you."

"Oh." Brian looked from Nathan to Gwen, unspoken curiosity lighting his eyes. "As you can see," he said to his sister, "I'm okay." Then without another word he turned with the clear intention of making for his room.

"Hold it! Where have you been?" Gwen demanded.

Brian shrugged. "Out."

"Out *where?*" She raised her hands, palms heavenward, her level of frustration impossible to contain. "Brian, you've got school tomorrow. You should have been here doing your homework long ago. Dinner is ruined. You left no message telling me where you were going or who you'd be with. What is going on with you? You've never done anything like this before."

There was pointed accusation in her tone. She heard it. But there wasn't a thing she could do about it. Anxiety had taken control.

His red hair, with its wiry texture, was sticking out in several directions. He was sweaty and grimy. But Gwen was too upset to remark on his physical appearance.

His face turned crimson. Being reprimanded in front of Nathan, whom he barely knew, embarrassed him, that much was evident.

"I'm going to bed," he declared. "Like you said, I have school tomorrow."

He moved to duck around her, but she planted herself in front of him.

"Oh, no, you don't." She glared at him. "You're not walking away from this. You're going to tell me who you've been with, where you've been and what you've been doing."

"I don't have to tell you nothin'."

Correcting his grammar never even entered her head. She was too overwhelmed by the injury his disrespectful tone of voice caused her.

"You're not my boss," he went on. "I'm old enough to come and go as I please."

For several seconds Gwen was so shocked she couldn't get her tongue to work. But then it loosened. Oh, boy! Did it ever loosen.

"You're thirteen years old. I'm responsible for you. Besides that, we're a family, Brian. I don't go off without telling you where I am, what I'm doing, when I'll be home. I think I deserve the same consideration from you."

Had that loud and angry lecture really spewed from her throat? What must Nathan think of her? She felt as if her mind and her body were no longer her own. Frustration and impatience had taken her hostage.

"I'm not talkin' about this!" Brian asserted hotly.

Refusing to meet her gaze, he shouldered his way around her, and Gwen was aware of the stench of cigarette smoke clinging to him. She opened her mouth to call him back, but Nathan's hand on her shoulder quieted her.

"Let him go," he quietly suggested.

The gentle pressure of his fingers calmed her, and that idea was comforting to her. Strange. Unexplainable. Definitely out of the ordinary for her. Yet comforting, nonetheless.

Brian's bedroom door latch clicked closed.

"That boy is going to make me lose my mind," she whispered.

She turned, her gaze falling on Nathan's face for the first time since her brother had returned home. Instantly she remembered the churning heat that had surrounded them as he'd held her close, and awk-wardness descended on her like a thick, immobilizing fog.

Nathan, on the other hand, didn't seem the least bit discomfited.

"Continuing this conversation with him now will only escalate the argument," he said. "At least you know he's safe."

Gwen sighed. That much was true.

"Now that I know he's okay," she quipped, "how many years would I spend in jail if I strangled him for making me worry so?"

He laughed out loud, and the sound of it broke the tension pent up inside her. She grinned.

"Raising kids these days is tough," he allowed.

"You don't know the half of it."

He looked at her quizzically and she knew he wanted her to elaborate. But she didn't know him well enough to be laying out her life story for him.

"Let me just say that my brother didn't have very good role models in his life." After a moment she softly added, "I just hope he's not going down the wrong path."

Nathan's brow smoothed. "It looked to me as if he was acting just like any other rebellious teen would."

Oh, if only she could be certain that was true. "You really think so?"

"I do."

He offered her a half smile, and Gwen was struck with the notion that it was the sexiest thing she'd ever seen in her life.

He continued, "I'll bet my last dollar that tomorrow morning, he'll apologize for coming in late. You mark my words."

His face brightened and he reached around to pull his wallet from his hip pocket.

"One of the first things I did when I came to the rez," he told her, "was to start a single parents group. We meet at the Community Center." He handed her a card. "You're more than welcome to attend the meetings."

She balked. "But I'm not Brian's mother, I'm his sister—"

"Doesn't matter," he cut her off. "You said it yourself just a moment ago. You're responsible for him. You're raising him on your own."

"Well…"

"Just think about it," he said. "It's good to have others to talk to."

Silence tumbled down around them as they exchanged a long, silent look. The stiffness Gwen had felt before returned full force. She couldn't keep her gaze on his face.

Her smile seemed plastic-coated. "Well, thank you for stopping by to check on us. I really appreciate it."

"I'm the sheriff. Checking up on people is what I do."

However, Gwen couldn't help but identify the hope swelling in her heart that there was more to his presence here tonight than his merely doing his job.

After he'd said good-night and Gwen was alone in her small living room, she thought about all that had happened. That odd, breathtaking heat she'd felt when Nathan had held her against him. The way his touch had calmed her when she'd felt such frustration at her brother's refusal to tell her where he'd been.

Nathan stirred something in her. Something amazing, something mysterious…

Then the stern, self-preserving voice in her head turned scolding. *You don't know Nathan Thunder. He's a stranger. It's terribly unwise for you to trust a man you don't know.*

She'd been hurt by men she'd loved in the past. Hurt beyond measure. Her father. Her stepfather. Men who hadn't deserved the trust she'd so innocently placed in their hands.

It would be best for her to stay away from Nathan. He made her feel things she didn't understand. He made her—

A thump from Brian's room had Gwen blinking her way out of the foggy haze of her thoughts and looking down the hallway at her brother's closed bedroom door. Apprehension crept over her. She loved her brother, but acting as Brian's guardian often overwhelmed her. Sure she taught six-year-olds, but what did she know about raising a teen? And with Brian's background, she had more than the normal teen problems with which to contend.

It sure would be nice to have somewhere to go for advice. Somewhere to turn for help.

It's good to have others to talk to. Nathan's words beamed through her muddled thoughts like a small ray of hope, warming and bright.

Trepidation rose inside her, snuffing out the warmth. Fear of trusting clawed at her. Nathan was a man, and she'd learned over the course of her life that it wasn't judicious for women to rely on men. It just wasn't. They'd fail you, again and again.

In the end, she tucked Nathan's card in the letter box by the phone, firming her resolve. She didn't need a man solving her problems. She could work them out herself. If she put her mind to it, she could.

Chapter Three

Gwen stood outside the Community Center the following Thursday evening, unable to deny the trepidation that congealed in her stomach like a lump of cold oatmeal. Would she be accepted by the other attendees once it was revealed that she was not a parent, but the sibling of the child she was responsible for? *Maybe it wouldn't make any difference,* a calm voice silently crooned. But then she remembered just how judgmental people could be.

She'd told Nathan last week she wouldn't come to the meeting. She'd told herself she could solve her own problems. So why had she hunted for the card he'd given her to discover the meeting details? Why had she walked across the reservation to the Community Center?

Her steps slowed until they stopped altogether.

As she tarried, refusing to face the honest-to-goodness truth, she couldn't help but admire the year-old stone-and-wood structure. When Gwen had accepted the job as first-grade teacher here on Smoke Valley Reservation, she'd read all the books she could find on the Kolheek, its culture and its history. She'd been interested in the rez itself, too. The principal of the rez school, Mrs. Halley, was full-blooded Kolheek and had been happy to take Gwen on a tour. Mrs. Halley had explained how there hadn't been an architect living at Smoke Valley when plans for the Community Center had been first brought up by the tribe's Council of Elders. But a granddaughter of one of the Elders, a young woman living in the Midwest, was working as an architectural engineer, and she had eagerly agreed to travel to Vermont to design the new building.

The rock had been hewn right from the mountainside, the timber harvested from the thick forests of the reservation. When Gwen had entered the building for the first time, she remembered marveling at how the outside of the structure was circular, yet the meeting rooms inside gave the illusion of being square—or nearly so. Yet at the very center of the building was a huge, round auditorium, a platform at its core, a high, domed ceiling overhead.

There was no doubt that the Community Center was an impressive building. Mrs. Halley had boasted, as only a native of the rez could, about how inexpensively the tribe had built the structure, most of the materials having come from Kolheek land and all the decorations having been donated by local Native American artisans.

"Well," Gwen whispered into the silky autumn night, "you're not doing yourself a bit of good just standing here on the sidewalk."

She hadn't placed her trust in a man for a very long time. But over the past few days she'd discovered that this problem with Brian was bigger than she could handle on her own. She needed help. And to get it, she was going to have to step out in faith. This was for Brian, she reminded herself. Forcing herself to put one foot in front of the other, she opened the front door and entered the center.

A small poster sat on an easel welcoming newcomers to the single parents group and informing them of the room number where the group was meeting. A big, black arrow pointed the way.

Gwen heard the rich timbre of Nathan's voice before she saw him. She stood in the doorway, her feet suddenly rooted to the smooth, wood-plank floor.

He stood, tall and proud, behind a podium at the front of the room, but he wasn't wearing his police uniform tonight. Instead, he had on a knitted crewneck sweater in hues of brown and rust. The collar of his tan shirt lay against his corded neck.

The sight of him both calmed her and excited her. And—yet again—she was amazed by the conglomeration of emotions the man incited in her.

Suddenly she realized Nathan had gone quiet. Then she realized his intense gaze had zeroed in on her. She felt heat rush to her face.

"Gwen," he called, "welcome. Come in and join us." He addressed the group. "Everyone, this is Gwen Fleming. Let's make her feel welcome."

As an elementary schoolteacher, Gwen routinely conducted quick headcounts throughout her workday. In the lunch room. At recess. Automatically now, as faces turned to stare, she counted a dozen people.

Even though some of the attendees smiled in greeting, the heat in Gwen's cheeks licked at her like tongues of fire.

"Sorry if I'm late," she murmured, dipping her head and hurrying to take a seat in the back row of metal folding chairs.

"No need to apologize," Nathan said easily. "I haven't been talking long." He gave her tonight's topic: how to tell if a teen is using drugs. And he summarized the points he'd made before her arrival before continuing.

As he spoke, every ounce of Gwen's attention became riveted to the man. He was knowledgeable on the subject, making it clear that it was his special training and experience with juveniles while working with the NYPD that made him so.

Once he'd completed his talk, the group shifted their chairs into a circle and took turns discussing their own personal situations. One woman made no apologies about ransacking her daughter's room when the teen wasn't at home.

"I need to know what she's up to," the woman said. "She refuses to talk to me, so I've got to take measures into my own hands."

The man across from her looked horrified. "But what will you do if she catches you in her room going through her things? I want to foster a trusting relationship between me and my kids. I'm sorry, but I think what you're doing is wrong."

Gwen listened as the two argued their positions, finally agreeing to disagree on the subject. The other parents chimed in with opinions now and then, as well. Gwen hadn't even thought of going through Brian's personal belongings to find clues about with whom he'd been spending his time or where he'd been going or what he'd been doing. She didn't know how she felt about the suggestion. Would it be an invasion of Brian's privacy? Gwen could see both sides of the argument.

Soon the meeting was over and Nathan was thanking everyone for coming and announcing the topic for the next meeting. Before she'd even had time to gather together her purse and the notes she'd taken, Nathan approached her.

"I'm glad you came," he said, sincerity expressed in his mahogany gaze.

She smiled, but the icy-hot feeling rushing over every inch of her skin seemed to paralyze her tongue. Feeling pressured to say something, anything, she blurted, "You sure seem organized for having just started this group. You gave such an informative talk. It must be a great deal of work to come up with a presentation each and every week—"

"Oh, I don't always do the talking." He chuckled. "I'm a pretty smart guy, but I'm not *that* smart."

Gwen couldn't help but laugh with him. She found it appealing to learn that he had the kind of self-confidence it took to make self-deprecating jokes. She thought it charming that Nathan could laugh at himself.

"I only gave the talk tonight," he continued, "because I have some experience with teens and drug use. Like I said, I worked with inner-city teens in New York. Next week I have a counselor lined up to discuss getting your kid to open up. Lots of people have that problem."

His eyes clouded, and Gwen got the distinct impression that he was thinking of his own relationship with his daughter, Charity, but before she could ask the questions that rolled into her head, he spoke again.

"Many weeks we won't be able to have a speaker at all," he told her. "You see, we can't afford to pay, so we have to rely on experts' willingness to volunteer their time to talk to us." His eyes lit up. "Hey, you'd make a great speaker. You could talk about ways to keep kids interested in their schoolwork. And how to get them to do their homework."

Her knee-jerk reaction was to refuse, but before she could, he smiled and rushed to say, "I'm sorry. I shouldn't attack you like that, this being your first night and all. I'll wait a few meetings and then ask again." Light laughter rumbled from deep in this throat. "Please forgive me. It's just that I'm excited about the single parents group."

There was no need to forgive him, Gwen realized. She found Nathan's excitement very alluring, indeed.

He sobered suddenly. "So...I must tell you, I was surprised to look up and see you standing in the door. When I talked to you last week, you said you wouldn't feel comfortable coming to the meeting. What happened to change your mind?"

His question was like having the rug pulled out from under her. She guessed it didn't take a rocket scientist to figure out that something had happened between her and Brian for her to change her opinion of attending the meeting. Still, his concern touched her in a way she'd never expected to be touched.

Right in the heart.

Nathan's tone lowered. "You want to talk about it?"

Suddenly Gwen felt as if she'd been holding her breath for days and days, and only just this moment was able to take a deep lungful of air.

"I'd love to talk."

"Good," he said. "Give me a second to lock up, and we'll walk across the street to the coffee shop."

Just after he'd ordered coffee for them both, Gwen began to talk. And she talked. And talked. And talked. It seemed to Nathan that the woman had never had anyone offer to listen before.

"So, you see," she said, adding a teaspoon of sugar and a dollop of cream to the second round of steaming coffee the waitress set down on the table, "Brian and I both had domineering fathers. Mine was verbally abusive, ridiculing and scornful." She sighed. "It was almost as if he enjoyed tearing strips off the people he was supposed to love."

Now, Nathan didn't know Gwen's father, had never met the man and probably never would. But seemingly out of nowhere, he felt this gargantuan urge to punch the man square in the nose. How could anyone be cruel to someone as delicate as Gwen? She was like a fragile piece of china that needed to be set high on a shelf somewhere safe and out of reach of the cold and harmful world.

"My father left us when I was just about ten. My mother sobbed as if he'd died. I didn't understand that. I was happy. I remember jumping up and down on my mattress with glee. This might be horrible, but I prayed that, wherever it was he went, he'd stay there. Mother and I lived on our own for a year or so. Then she married Robert." She sighed. "And life as I knew it changed forever."

Memories drew deep and disturbing lines on Gwen's forehead. Nathan fought the urge to reach across the table and smooth the pad of his thumb across them. He didn't know what changes this Robert brought into her life, but it was clear that they weren't good.

She was silent for quite a while. Then she seemed to become conscious of the silence, most uncomfortable with it, actually.

"We muddled through," she whispered. Her tone grew stronger. "Mom had Brian. I stayed out of the way as much as I could." Her smile didn't hold much humor. "A kid can become pretty adept at that."

Unwittingly she bent her elbow, lifting her fingers, worrying them over her lips. Nathan became mesmerized by the movement. Began dreaming of what it might feel like to pull her fingertips from her mouth and…kiss those perfect lips.

Keep your thoughts on the conversation at hand, a stern voice in the back of his brain chided him.

Then he noticed the emotion that darkened her clear, green eyes. She might be explaining flashes of her childhood, but it was obvious to him that he would probably never know all that she'd experienced.

"It was such a relief to go off to college," she finally said. "I feel guilty saying this, but I felt free for the first time in my life. I couldn't bring myself to go back home. So I found a job during the summer, and I stayed in that small, quaint college town."

Her voice grew hushed and she seemed to have difficulty meeting his gaze.

"Even after Mom died," she said, "I couldn't go back. I found one excuse after another to stay away. Robert was just so…hard. So mean-spirited. After my mother passed away, my stepfather refused to help me with tuition. So I earned that myself. Money was tight, but I did it. I graduated."

Nathan saw that her hands were actually trembling as she lifted the mug to her mouth for a sip. His empathy was almost too big for him to contain. It swelled until his chest burned from its volume.

"Once I began teaching," she continued, "once I

had some steady income coming in, I went to see Brian.''

Emotion welled in her eyes and Nathan thought his heart would split in two. Reaching out, he covered her hand with his.

''Robert was abusing my brother.''

She squeezed the words from her throat with difficulty.

''He was taking out his frustrations on Brian's back. With a belt. The welts were…''

Her eyelids closed and she obviously couldn't finish. But there was no need for her to. Nathan understood perfectly. In his line of work, he frequently encountered abusive parents.

''I'm sorry, Gwen. I'm sorry this happened to Brian. No one should have to endure that kind of treatment. Especially a defenseless kid.''

Her inhalation was shaky. ''That's exactly what I thought. So I took him away from there.''

He couldn't stop the surprise from showing on his face. Luckily Gwen was too lost in her story to notice.

''I don't know what I'd have done without Mattie Russell,'' she told him. ''She put us up at her bed-and-breakfast.'' Her smile went taut, as if she was suddenly very conscious of her words. Softly she murmured, ''Mattie's been an angel sent straight from above.''

Nathan only smiled. As sheriff, he knew all about Mattie Russell and her dedication to those who found themselves with no way out.

Gwen glanced out the window, her index finger and

thumb absently moving up and down the handle of the heavy, white crockery.

Caring about this woman wasn't something Nathan wanted to do. With Charity, he had enough problems of his own right now. But he couldn't deny that he felt drawn to Gwen.

"Hey, you seem so far away right now." He smiled when his soft words succeeded in gaining her attention. The clouds in her gem-green eyes tore at his heart.

"Thanks for listening," she said.

His grin widened. "Anytime." Then he slid his fingertips over the back of her warm, silken hand. Contact with her made fireworks erupt in his chest. He did what he could to ignore them. "But, Gwen, you never said what it was that made you come to the meeting tonight. You never said what it was that changed your mind."

She looked down into her mug, then tipped up her chin and met his gaze.

Finally she said, "Just as you said, Brian woke up the next morning and apologized for being out late."

Nathan remained silent, knowing instinctively that there was more to the story.

"But he refused to talk to me," she rushed to add. "He wouldn't tell me where he goes or who he hangs out with. He was keeping me in the dark and I didn't, don't like it." Gwen averted her gaze. "So I pushed him. Nagged at him until he just blew up again. We fought. Horribly." A heavy sigh rushed from her. "I'm worried, Nathan. Brian's behavior could be a simple case of teenage rebellion, as you suggested. But then again, this could be leading to something...something really bad.''

Nathan couldn't keep silent. ''You're not feeling threatened by him, are you? Physically threatened, I mean?''

''No,'' she said. ''I don't believe my brother would ever lay a hand on me. But he's so full of bitterness and anger. I don't know how to get him to release it.''

Oh, Great One, Nathan prayed, *give me the right words to say. Help me to know what to do to help her.*

''That's why I'm here, Nathan. For Brian. I want to learn what I can do to help him heal.''

She looked utterly defenseless, and Nathan was walloped with the urge to protect her. To swoop in and take care of all her tribulations.

Just then, something inside rose up and hit him...hit him hard, warning him not to get too involved with Gwen and her troubled brother, warning him he had enough problems of his own, warning him that he didn't need more difficulty on top of what he already had.

Without further thought, he plucked a pen and card from his breast pocket and jotted down his home phone number. He should be marveling at his behavior—a cop never gave out his home number—but some higher calling told him this was different. This was necessary.

''I don't know what I can do to help you, Gwen,''

he said. The air between them seemed to grow as soft as her expression. "But I can promise that if you need me, I *will* be there."

Gwen watched Nathan approach the school from the office window. The worried expression on his handsome face squeezed her heart. She probably could have handled this situation with Charity on her own. No, she *knew* she could have. It was just that, well...the man had been so kind to her after the single parents meeting. He'd shown her such compassion. And besides, she hadn't been able to think of much of anything but him since then.

"Admit it," she muttered under her breath, "you simply wanted to see the man."

And Charity had given her a prime opportunity to do just that.

"Pardon?"

The school secretary's voice took Gwen aback. "Oh, nothing." She smiled self-consciously. "I was just talking to myself."

The elderly woman grinned. "Working with children will often have a body doing that."

Nathan pushed open the front door and came into the office.

"Thanks for coming," Gwen said in greeting. Her heart tripped a staccato beat against her ribs. He was such a good-looking man with those intense, deep-set eyes, that silky hair, those high cheekbones.

He nodded in response, then asked, "Where is she?"

"With Mrs. Halley. In the teachers' lounge."
Gwen hoped the quirky smile she offered would alleviate some of his obvious anxiety. "We thought we should keep Charity at the scene of the crime, so to speak."

He grinned, then shook his head. "I can't believe that my daughter's become a thief."

Gwen grimaced as she led him up the hallway. "That's a harsh way to describe her behavior."

"You told me on the phone that she pilfered doughnuts from the teachers' lounge. To pilfer is to steal."

"Well...maybe," Gwen said. "But that description still sounds too severe to me."

They paused a moment outside the door leading to the lounge. She asked him, "You ready?"

He sighed. "As ready as I'll ever be, I guess. Dealing with that little minx is going to drive me around the bend."

Her mouth pulled back at the corners. "Hold firm. And remember you have lots of supporters."

Without thinking, she reached out and slid comforting fingers over his biceps. The hardness of muscle nearly had her sucking in her breath, and heated tendrils sprouted to life deep in her gut. She snatched her hand from his arm and quickly focused on grabbing the doorknob and pushing her way into the lounge.

The school's principal was standing with one hip leaning on the edge of the table, her arms tightly crossed over her chest. The frustration on Mrs. Halley's face told Gwen that the woman hadn't had much success in getting Charity, who was sitting on a chair in front of her, to recognize the error of her ways. Why, the child hadn't even felt self-conscious enough to wipe the powdered sugar from the corners of her mouth.

It was Mrs. Halley's policy to allow teachers to handle their students' disciplinary problems whenever possible. Gwen liked that the principal's philosophy was based on the idea of not having the children feel ganged up on by adults, so after nodding to Nathan and Gwen, Mrs. Halley left the lounge.

"What are you doing in the teachers' lounge, young lady?" Nathan asked his daughter once the door was closed.

"Like I told Mrs. Halley, the teachers had doughnuts." The child's tone clearly conveyed that she thought this fact was reason enough, and Gwen had to control the smile that threatened to crack across her face.

"You couldn't possibly have been hungry this morning," Nathan asserted. "I fixed pancakes for breakfast. You polished off three. Not to mention the two helpings of applesauce you ate."

Charity leaned forward, and as though speaking to a blubbering idiot, she slowing enunciated, "We're talkin' *doughnuts,* Dad."

Gwen's eyes rounded, her gaze flying to Nathan. She thought she saw steam rolling heavenward from his ears as anger darkened his expression. Then he evidently noticed something.

"Is that a coffee stain on your top?" Without waiting for an answer, he pointed at Charity. "You helped yourself to a cup of coffee, didn't you? What were you thinking?"

"I was thinkin' that doughnuts taste real good when they're dunked in coffee."

Gwen thought Nathan's head would explode with frustration.

"But you're not allowed to drink coffee!"

Charity's bottom lip quivered suddenly, and tears sprang to her eyes. But Gwen suspected it wasn't because she realized what she'd done was wrong, but that Nathan had raised his voice.

Confusion knitted her tiny brow as she wailed, "But I always used to have coffee in my city life. And you never said I couldn't have no coffee. And nobody told me I couldn't have no doughnut, either."

The room went totally quiet. Gwen couldn't help but find it very interesting that the child didn't just think of her pre-Nathan existence as another time, but a whole other life.

"The point is, Charity—" Nathan's tone was controlled "—the teachers' lounge is for *teachers*. You are a student, not a teacher. You do not belong in here."

The girl crossed her little arms over her chest, her chin tipping up as she pointed out, "Well, if they don't want anybody in here, then they shouldn't have coffee and doughnuts where us kids can smell 'em."

"That's enough, young lady."

Again Nathan's firm tone had his daughter's face crumpling.

"You lose television privileges for a week because of this. And another thing, I don't care if you smell doughnuts or filet mignon, you are not to come in here again. Do you understand?"

Charity nodded, subdued now.

The confrontation over, Gwen felt it was her turn to take control. "Charity, why don't you go to the rest room and wash your face with cool water? I'll meet you back at the classroom, okay?"

"Yes, ma'am." She slid off the chair and made her way to the door. She turned back to face them after she'd opened it. "Dad, I'm sorry. I didn't mean to make you mad at me."

"Honey, everyone makes mistakes," he told her gently. "The important thing is that we don't repeat them."

"You don't have to worry about me coming in here if I smell that filly stuff," she rushed to assure him. "I don't even know what that is." Her eyes grew pained. "It's the doughnuts that are dangerous."

The door closed, and Gwen and Nathan were alone in the lounge. The sound of his soulful sigh was heart-wrenching.

"What am I going to do with that child?" he asked softly.

Without thinking, she slid her fingertips over the corded muscles of his forearm. Tiny shocks of electric current zipped and ricocheted through the fabric of his uniform. The very air seemed to tighten. He noticed it. She knew he did.

The two of them stood for several seconds, seemingly unable to speak.

Gwen's mouth went as dry as cotton and she moistened her lips. His eyes were glued to her mouth. She swallowed.

Her students were waiting. As much as she'd like to indulge in these heated moments of...of... whatever this was, she simply couldn't. She had a job to do.

To lighten the mood, she quipped, "Doughnuts *are* pretty dangerous."

She was glad when she saw him smile, and she gave his arm a reassuring squeeze. "We'll stand as a united front, you and I. We'll soon teach her the rules. You'll see."

"It isn't just how she overlooks the rules." His whole face seemed to fall a fraction. "It's...well, it's everything. She's such a tomboy. She has no interest whatsoever in normal girl things. Dolls. Or pretty clothes. Or anything else, well, feminine."

Gwen felt suddenly pressed for time. "Nathan, I'd love to talk about this, but—" she glanced at her watch "—the morning bell is about to ring. I have—"

"Gwen, I'm sorry," he said. "I sure didn't mean to keep you. Oh, but one thing before you go—I've been thinking about Brian. I'd like to invite the two of you to the Harvest Celebration. It's a Kolheek tradition. I think you'll enjoy yourselves."

The thought of spending the evening with Nathan made her belly churn with excitement. She'd read about the celebration and wondered if she'd get the opportunity to attend. "I'd love to go," she told him. "I'm sure Brian would, too."

"It's also Kolheek tradition for the men to spend the weekend hunting," Nathan said. "I thought that Brian might like to come along with me. We'll do some tracking and fishing. We'll make our own shelter. A couple of days providing for himself might, I don't know, help your brother to gain some self-respect. He can't respect others unless he respects himself, you know?"

"Nathan—" she couldn't believe how enamored of this man she was becoming "—that sounds like it would be a wonderful experience for Brian. If you're sure this is something you want to take on."

He was quiet for a second. Then he said, "I wouldn't have offered if I didn't."

The temperature in the room seemed to heat up, and the air felt tight again.

All Gwen could say was "Thanks."

The school bell rang, yet neither of them moved.

Nathan's dark gaze seemed to light with a sudden idea. "Hey, maybe you could spend the weekend with my daughter. Teach her some soft, womanly things. Like baking a pie. Or shopping for a dress."

She couldn't stop the grin that crept over her lips. "So baking a pie is a womanly thing, huh?"

"Well…"

She laughed as embarrassment flamed his swarthy handsome face.

"You know what I mean."

Gwen nodded. "I do. And I'd love to swap kids with you this weekend. But I have to tell you, I think we both have formidable tasks ahead of us."

"We can handle them, though, don't you think?"

He didn't expect an answer, she knew that.

"So, I'll see you at the celebration Friday night?" he asked.

She nodded. And as she watched him walk away, she marveled at how warm and mushy her heart had grown. He was kind. And concerned. He was honorable. And well respected in this community of Kolheeks.

She couldn't think of a better role model for her brother than Nathan Thunder.

Chapter Four

The old shaman made his way into the center of the crowd. Gwen was in awe at the sudden and respectful silence that settled around her. The Harvest Celebration had been buzzing with the laughter of adults, the squeals and shouts of running children, but now the large group went utterly still, and the only sounds that could be heard were the snap and hiss of the large bonfire and the chirping of the night insects.

"Life is a cycle," Joseph Thunder announced in his commanding timbre. "An endless, ever-flowing circle. It is said that in the beginning Kit-tan-it-to'wet, the Great Spirit, made the world and placed creatures upon the good, dry land and in the deep seas. Among those creatures was Toad, who was given the responsibility of the waters. He kept them in his body, letting them out only as they were needed to moisten

Mother Earth, to keep her oceans full, her rivers running swiftly.''

Every eye was on the elderly man. Gwen let her gaze rove over his impressive traditional garb. His shoulder-length, steel-gray hair hung loose, confined only by a fancy beaded headband. The leather tunic he wore was hand-tooled. His leggings, which looked to be made of tanned animal skin, had an ornate beaded design on each thigh and were fastened down the sides with thongs that lent a fringed effect. The moccasins covering his feet were unadorned, the cuff flaps so large that they nearly brushed the ground around his heels.

''One day,'' Joseph continued, his rich voice weaving itself warmly through the crowd, ''a wicked horned serpent appeared and fought with Toad. The monster gored Toad in the side and water surged, threatening to overflow Mother Earth.''

Darting a quick glance at her brother, Gwen saw that he was held as rapt by the ancient legend as the rest of those gathered around the fire. She smiled, realizing that children of all ages enjoyed a well-told tale, and Joseph was certainly proving to be a mesmerizing storyteller.

''A powerful man named Nan'a-push—'' the shaman's words once again pulled at Gwen's attention ''—lived on the earth, and when he saw the rising water, he raced toward the highest mountain he could find. With each swift step he took, he gathered up animals, tucking them into the bosom of his belted robe.''

Suddenly Gwen was overcome with a prickly sensation. Sensing eyes on her, she turned her head, and her gaze collided with Nathan's. The intensity of his stare made her body flush hotly. Since the moment she'd arrived, she'd been terribly aware that something magical heated the night. She'd thought it was the excitement of the evening, the electricity that seemed to pulse from the mood of the people. However, as she stood here, her gaze tangling sensuously with Nathan's, she couldn't help but feel that the mysterious tension glittering and dancing in the air had a much more personal origin. Finally she tore her gaze away from the man who filled her thoughts, who stirred in her an aching yet unnamable need, and she focused on the shaman.

"At the very top of the mountain," Joseph continued, "was a cedar tree. When the water reached the top of the mountain, Nan'a-push began to climb the tree. He reached the top of the tree, but the water was unrelenting. Nan'a-push began to sing, beating in time with an arrow upon his bowstring. As he sang, the tree began to grow. The cedar continued to grow as the waters rose, so that the waves never quite reached the man's feet."

A covert peek at Nathan told Gwen he was no longer staring at her. She was relieved...and terribly disappointed.

The shaman said, "Finally Nan'a-push tired of singing, and he pulled off some of the tree's branches and tossed them onto the water, creating a strong raft. He and the animals floated until all the earth was swallowed by water. After a while, Nan'a-push decided that a new Mother Earth should be made, a task he knew he could perform through the power that had been granted to him by Kit-tan-it-to'wet.''

"That—" Gwen started when she heard Nathan's voice so close to her ear for she hadn't even heard him approach her from behind "—is my favorite part of the story." His sweet breath tickled her neck. "I like thinking that the Great One would bestow such power on a mere human."

A shiver coursed down her spine when she suddenly realized that Nathan—mere human that he was—held amazing power…over *her*.

"However," Joseph said to the crowd, "Nan'a-push needed a small bit of Mother Earth to start with. So he sent the loon, who dived deep to get a little mud. Loon stayed under the water a long time."

The very night seemed to wait in breathless anticipation.

"When he came floating back to the surface, he was dead. Nan'a-push breathed life back into loon. Next, he sent otter. Otter tried to reach the bottom, but he, too, died. Nan'a-push revived him. Next was beaver's turn, with the same result, but Nan'a-push revived him, as well. Finally, muskrat made one last attempt. His lifeless body floated to the surface, but he was able to gather a bit of mud in his mouth and paws before he died. Nan'a-push breathed muskrat back to life and blessed him, telling him that he was favored among animals and that his tribe would never die out."

Keeping her attention on the story being told was difficult for Gwen. The heated spicy scent of Nathan wafted around her. She could feel the solidness of him just behind her left shoulder, and it took every bit of her willpower not to surrender to the urge to lean against him.

"Now Nan'a-push needed one of the creatures to carry the earth." Joseph paused, looking around the crowd. "Turtle stepped forward, and the mud was placed on his back. It began to grow until it was a large island. It expanded into the land we live on today."

Joseph Thunder fell silent. Apparently the Kol-heeks knew this was the end of the story, for the dreamlike stillness was soon broken with movement and quiet discussion.

"What a wonderful story," Gwen said. Mustering a brilliant smile, she tried to hide the breathlessness she felt at Nathan's nearness.

He nodded, then looked at Brian. "So what did you think of my grandfather's tale?"

The teen just shrugged. "It was neat. It was also a lot like the biblical story of Noah, the guy who built the ark."

"Yes," Nathan said. "It's amazing how many cultures have some kind of story that revolves around a great flood."

"I've heard of Noah," Charity said. "That story ends with a big rainbow."

"That's right. It does." Nathan smiled down at the child.

"I r-really like," Brian haltingly added, "how the man in the story referred to the muskrat as being, well, part of a tribe. Like the muskrat was, I dunno, on the same level as the man, rather than being—" he hitched a shoulder "—less than the man or something."

Gwen was surprised by Brian's insightful observation. Nathan, she saw, seemed impressed by it, too.

"We believe," Nathan said softly, "that all forms of life deserve our respect. It's something that's taught to us from the very start of our lives. No being is higher than another."

A momentary shadow passed across Brian's gaze, and Gwen was left wondering what might be going through his mind.

Nathan said, "But my grandfather didn't quite finish the story."

"Oh?" Gwen's curiosity was piqued.

"It is Kolheek tradition for the shaman to leave this particular tale unfinished," Nathan informed them. "This gives the People a chance to practice the Oral Tradition themselves. This practice is especially important for parents of young children."

Sure enough, Gwen glanced around and saw that everyone had gathered in small groups, their heads bent in conversation.

"So," Brian was quick to pipe up, "how does the rest of the story go?"

Nathan picked up Charity. "Well…I hope I can get this right. It's been a while since I've told this tale." He cleared his throat. "Once Mother Earth was restored, every so often Nan'a-push would send a wolf to see how large the new land had grown. The first time the wolf left and returned in one day. The second time, the wolf didn't return for five days. The third time, it took ten days. Then it took the length of a moon cycle. Then a year. And then five years. It is said that the last time Nan'a-push checked to see how big Mother Earth had grown, he sent a young wolf, but the wolf died of old age before it could return. That is when Nan'a-push felt that the earth was large enough and commanded it to stop growing. Now, it is believed that Nan'a-push lives far to the north and that he sleeps all winter like the bear. Before he goes to bed, he smokes a big stone pipe. When the air fills with blue smoke in the fall, everyone knows Nan'a-push is getting ready for bed and that winter is coming.''

Simultaneously all eyes went heavenward, searching the night sky for smoky clouds, and Gwen smiled. Her heart felt happy to have had this opportunity to experience the rich tapestry that was Kolheek tradition.

''I have a question.'' Charity tugged on Nathan's earlobe to get his attention.

''And what is that?'' Nathan asked, smiling at her.

Gwen braced herself for the child's inquiry. Would she question how a toad could hold enough water in its body to flood the earth? Would she dispute that a man could make a tree grow by singing? Or that smoke from a stone pipe could fill the whole sky with clouds?

"How come great-grandfather is wearing those funny clothes?"

Nathan chuckled at his daughter's query. As he lowered her to the ground, he said, "Why don't you go ask him for yourself?"

Charity scampered off toward Joseph.

"I'm starving," Brian said. "Are they serving the food yet?"

"If not," Nathan told him, "they'll be serving it soon. The food tables are over that way."

Gwen watched her brother jog off.

Once again the shaman raised a hand to garner the crowd's attention. He proudly held young Charity in his other arm.

"Last spring," he said, "we fed Mother Earth and prayed that the Great Spirit would bless us with a bountiful harvest. Today we celebrate that harvest. Let us dance and sing and eat and show that we gratefully and joyfully enjoy all that we have been given!"

Immediately men in breechcloths and elaborate feathered headdresses encircled the fire, singing and dancing to the primitive beat of drums. Some people in the crowd stood to watch, others moved toward the tables that were laden with a bounty of delicious food. When Gwen passed the tables earlier, she'd seen roasted ears of corn, beans flavored with smoky bacon, fried chicken, venison stew, an assortment of salads, fresh-baked breads and traditional desserts sweetened with honey and molasses, and she'd been fascinated at the culinary variety.

"So," Nathan said, "is Brian ready for our weekend outing?"

Gwen tempered her nod with an uncertain grin. "He's trying hard to remain noncommittal about the trip." She chuckled. "It isn't cool for a kid his age to be looking forward to spending the weekend with an adult. But I can tell that he's excited about going. Robert wasn't an outdoorsman. He never took Brian fishing or camping."

"We'll have fun." Nathan shifted his weight. "And hopefully I'll get the chance to talk to him a little bit about growing up. About what it means to be a man. But don't worry. I won't be heavy-handed about it."

The fact that Nathan was willing to spend this time with her brother made Gwen feel terribly grateful. Usually people wanted nothing whatsoever to do with sullen, misbehaving teens. Brian had some really wonderful traits. He was a good kid with a good heart. She wanted to be optimistic in thinking that his positive characteristics would dominate the negative ones. Yet at the same time it could be that the abuse he'd suffered had left him with a chip on his shoulder that no one would be able to remove.

Nathan's chin dipped and he eyed her dubiously as he asked, "You ready for your weekend with Charity?"

Gwen was helpless against the laugh that bubbled from her. "Don't make it sound like I'm in taking on Attila the Hun, okay? Charity and I are going to have a great time. I've got all kinds of girlie things planned for us to do.''

It was obvious to her that he was feeling the same deep gratitude as she. Like tiny cat's paws, pleasure padded through her being. And it made her happy to think that they were helping each other out with their problems.

''Charity will be okay with Grandfather for a few minutes,'' Nathan said, glancing over his shoulder. He turned his dark gaze on Gwen. ''Would you like to take a walk?''

His handsome face took on an expression so packed with awareness that the molecules in the night air seemed to speed up, enveloping her in a delicious, anticipatory warmth.

''Sure.'' She spoke the word in a short, breathy whisper.

Something was about to happen. She could feel it down to the marrow of her bones.

Having grown up in a home with a verbally abusive father, Gwen had never remembered a time in her youth when she hadn't been frightened of men. She had never known when she was going to be ridiculed or mercilessly teased to tears. And because of that, she'd grown up withdrawn and fearful. The lesson she'd learned from that was, although it was better to be seen and not heard, it was best if you made yourself invisible.

Lucky for her, her mother's second husband had pretty much ignored Gwen. But her stepfather had been physically abusive toward his wife. Gwen had observed that behavior. She'd learned from it, too.

The moral of her life story was to steer clear of the opposite sex.

And she'd spent much of her teenage years doing just that. She never had a boyfriend all through high school. Not one. She'd just been too shy when it came to boys. Shy, nothing. She'd been afraid, plain and simple.

However, she'd been intelligent enough to finally figure out that not all guys were overbearing and mean-spirited. She spent the first two years of college just being friends with different young men. A couple of them had pushed for more, yes, but for the most part, she found her male friends to be fun-loving and understanding. Most of them were even kind and caring. Finally she'd garnered enough nerve to accept an honest-to-goodness date.

Oh, how nervous she'd been. But everything had turned out just fine.

Slowly she'd gotten over her fear of men. If not entirely, she'd at least learned to live with her trepidation. However, she'd never quite been able to wholly and unreservedly hand over her trust to a man.

Nathan had been a calm, stable and helpful presence from the very first day she'd met him. He'd taken Brian aside in that shop and given him a good talking-to when, by rights, he could have hauled her brother to the town jailhouse and charged him with shoplifting.

And the man was strong. Physically, yes, but what

she'd been more impressed with was his strength of character. He'd taken Charity in without blinking an eye. He'd been most happy to fulfill his obligation to his daughter. Some men would have bolted from the idea of raising a six-year-old alone.

Nathan was nothing at all like either her father or stepfather. That much was obvious. She'd never seen the man cross. Frustrated with his daughter's antics, yes. Angry, no. She'd never heard him use a ridiculing tone, even when little Charity had misbehaved abominably. Yes, it was clear that Nathan was the exact opposite of the men who had raised Gwen.

And the man was gorgeous as all get-out.

There was no denying the fact that she'd felt amazingly attracted to him from the very moment she'd first laid eyes on him. He made her insides churn with mysterious emotions. He stirred something in her, something she'd never before experienced.

When they entered the woods, his palm settled, warm, secure and snug, in hers.

"It's dark," Nathan warned, his voice as soft as the silky night, "and the path is uneven. Watch your step."

There was something wonderfully sensuous in his tone, and she couldn't say if it was the concern he expressed or just the gentleness of his voice. Her stomach felt as if it had suddenly come alive with dozens of fluttering butterflies.

Nathan tugged at her hand and she followed him under the drooping branches of a huge oak tree. He spun her around, and she felt the rough bark pressing into her back through the light jacket she wore. She could still hear the beat of the drums back at the celebration.

He was close. So close. His dark eyes swallowed her whole. The need she read in his gaze made her body glow with a delicious heat.

"I've fought this," he said, his speech ragged. "I've fought hard against what I'm feeling for you."

His words barely registered. All Gwen was cognizant of was the thumping of the drums and how the beat mirrored her own heartbeat. His hot, needy eyes pierced her to the very soul.

All she wanted to do was get lost in the ancient, primeval rhythm. To let the moment pick her up and carry her away. If Nathan didn't act on the palpable passion emanating from him, she was certain she wouldn't be able to stand it.

"Kiss me." There was an urgency in her whisper.

She wondered if the demand had really passed from her lips. This was so unlike her. But this night was unlike any other she'd ever experienced. This moment was unlike any other, as well. And this man...well, he certainly was unlike any other she'd ever met.

His mouth slanted down over hers, and her chest swelled with utter joy. Her eyelids lowered, and she nearly cried out with the pure pleasure that vibrated through her. His kiss was warm and moist and honey sweet. Unable to help herself, she reached up and wove her fingers deep into his sleek hair. Her chin was tipped up and his fingers traced the length of her throat. Her breath caught as a million pointy-tipped stars seemed to roll, end over end, across every inch of her skin.

He settled his hands on her waist, his touch warming the small of her back. He slowly, languorously explored the inner recesses of her mouth with his tongue, and Gwen was certain she'd faint dead away from the sheer pleasure coursing through her. His hands rose, higher and higher, pausing to linger at her rib cage, and adrenaline sent blood whooshing through her ears.

A shudder jolted through her when the pads of his thumbs grazed the tender undersides of her breasts, his lips playing, frolicking along her jaw. Then his hands were on her, cupping her fullness. He nipped gently at her earlobe, and Gwen thought that surely she'd suffocate in the sheer delight the sensation gave her.

At this moment in time, her whole world was Nathan. His scent filled her nostrils and lungs. His jagged breathing roared in her ears. The taste of him was still on her tongue. Her fingers roved through the satin of his hair, over the smoothness of his clean-shaven jaw. Every cell of her being was saturated with him.

He kneaded her breasts, and her nipples hardened into nubs. He dragged the pad of his thumb over one stiff bud, and even through the fabric of her jacket, blouse and bra, his touch felt so delicious that Gwen inhaled deeply, sharply.

Frantic to feel his touch on her bare skin, she reached up and drew down the zipper of her jacket in one swift motion. He kissed the curve of her neck, the heat of his breath like fiery silk against her flesh. With one hand, she worked to unfasten the top buttons of her blouse; however, frustration set in quickly.

"Here," he said, stilling her fumbling fingers with his, "let me."

With excruciating slowness, he unbuttoned her blouse. Gwen felt breathless as she waited...waited. He pushed aside the facings, letting his eyes rove over every inch of her lacy bra, the swell of her breasts. Her chest rose and fell, and his gaze felt as intense and real as a physical touch.

"Please," she said, her emotions running so high she wasn't sure her voice was even audible, "I want to feel your hands on me."

The wantonness throbbing through her was so new, so...freeing.

She felt safe with Nathan. Safer than she'd ever felt with another human being. Safe enough to reveal this most basic and overwhelming desire raging through her. Desire for him.

He traced the peach-laced edge of her bra, his index finger sketching lightly across her skin. Then he bent his head and kissed her, the swarthy tone of his jaw contrasting deeply with her own milky flesh.

Heat sprouted and curled like liquid smoke low in her belly. Closing her eyes, she simply enjoyed the feel of him.

"Dad!"

Nathan's head lifted and swiveled toward the sound of Charity's voice somewhere out there in the direction from which they had come. Before he answered, he directed his gaze at Gwen, and the disappointment she read there made her heart soar.

Over his shoulder, he called into the darkness, "I'm coming, honey. Stay on the path right where you are. I don't want you getting lost among the trees."

Immediately, he began helping Gwen straighten her blouse, fasten her buttons. He chuckled softly, his face close to hers.

"I feel like a teenager caught necking," he whispered.

Gwen just smiled. He actually looked embarrassed, and she found that too alluring for words.

At that moment she felt something happen inside her. A funny, heated hitch in her heart. Gwen had never been in love before. She'd never experienced the feeling of falling for a man. Of feeling as if she wouldn't mind spending the rest of the night with him…or maybe even the rest of her life with him. But if she had to hazard a guess, she'd have to say that the emotion humming through her was just that.

Love.

Chapter Five

The two days that Nathan spent with Gwen's teenage brother were the longest of his life. The time was not only exhausting, it was frustrating beyond belief.

The first several hours of Saturday morning had been wasted as Nathan waited for the batteries of Brian's portable cassette player to run out. Nathan had hoped to spend the first several hours getting to know the boy a little better, but it seemed the teen couldn't live without the music that blared from the earphones clamped on his head. In Nathan's mind communing with nature had nothing whatsoever to do with electronic gizmos, but pointing that out would only have alienated Brian, and that wasn't his goal. So he'd patiently waited, and once the batteries were dead, he'd smiled to himself and felt the trip had finally begun.

However, looking back on it now, Nathan couldn't help but come to the conclusion that their camping weekend had been doomed from the start. Although Brian had seemed interested, even curious, about Nathan's stories of his boyhood and how his grandfather had taken him on many such weekends as this, Nathan had had to admit that it had been a long time since he'd last fished and tracked game and lived off the land. And those years had evidently taken a heavy toll on his survival skills.

He and Brian had fished for hours without a nibble. Finally they'd given up on the idea of the lake providing their lunch. Nathan had found a rabbit's den, but Brian had looked squeamish at the idea of killing the furry creature. So Saturday evening the two of them, tired and ravenous, had tucked in to a dinner of Indian cucumbers, wild potatoes and the handful of berries Nathan had harvested from the forest.

And Brian had, at first, been quite impressed by Nathan's shelter-building skills. He'd watched with rapt attention as Nathan had stripped narrow bands of bark to be used as rope. They had soaked the bark strips in the lake to make them more pliable and then tied together bent saplings and layered on a covering of thick pine boughs.

The two of them were snuggled in their sleeping bags, protected from the cool of the autumn night, and Nathan was just dozing off when it came to their attention that they had built their makeshift shelter right on top of a nest of ants. The insects were swarming all over them and they had jumped up, performing something akin to the ancient Kolheek Rain Dance in their effort to brush the ants off themselves. In the moonlight, their gazes met. Nathan could tell Brian was trying hard not to laugh. Finally they both surrendered to the humor of their predicament.

After they had shaken the insects from their sleeping bags, they decided to simply sleep under the stars, rather than take the time to build another shelter.

One good thing had happened, Nathan thought. While the two of them had lain in the darkness, Brian had begun to talk about his past. Not a lot. But some. Enough for Nathan to realize that Brian was a bright kid who had had some rough knocks in his short life.

Under the inky sky, Nathan had fallen asleep Saturday night, too tired to react to the errant ant that crawled across his ankle.

Sunday morning, both Nathan and Brian awoke chilled to the bone.

"Come on," Nathan said. "Let's break camp and clean up our mess here. I know where we can go for a hot meal."

"But we're out in the middle of nowhere." Regardless of this observation, Brian had immediately begun to roll up his sleeping bag.

A short hike brought them to a cabin on the far side of Smoke Lake.

"Hey!" Nathan called out loudly.

Brian gave a start. "Why'd you do that?" he whispered. "You scared me to death."

"It's a hailing call. To let my cousin know we're approaching."

Brian looked askance. "I always thought that's what a knock on the front door was for."

Chuckling, Nathan lifted a shoulder and explained further. "Long ago, if you were to advance on someone's home without calling out first, they would assume you had nefarious intentions. Foes stalk silently while friends don't mind letting their presence be known." He tilted his head. "I guess you could call it an Indian custom. One that some of us continue to keep. Besides, it's good manners to let people know you're coming. Gives them time to get into the mindset of having visitors." He grinned. "For all we know, my cousin is inside taking a bath. This way he'll have time to find his pants."

"So, this is your cousin's place?" Brian asked.

"Well…" Nathan hesitated, not sure how much he should reveal about Conner and his problems. "Let's just say my cousin is staying here for a while."

"But it's so far from town." The boy was quiet as he scanned the area. "And it looks…well, primitive."

Nathan laughed. "That's a polite description if ever I heard one. The cabin has running water, but no electricity. It was used as a hunting lodge for years. A place where people could get out of the cold." Nathan decided Brian needed a little more information, so he added, "Conner is taking a small sabbatical."

"He's taking time off from a job? If I was going on a vacation, it wouldn't be to the middle of nowhere."

Nathan pondered. "Conner's not on vacation." Softly he said, "I guess you could say he's taking time off from life."

Curiosity lit the teen's eyes, but to Nathan's relief

the boy didn't get the chance to ask more questions, for they'd reached the porch and Conner had opened the front door. Nathan took the stairs two at a time.

"Nathan!"

"Conner!"

The two men embraced, thumping each other on the back affectionately.

"I'd like you meet Brian," Nathan said, urging the teen up the steps with a wave of his hand. He nearly introduced him as the brother of a friend, but after quick second thought, he said, "He's a new friend of mine."

He wasn't certain, but he thought he saw Brian cut a grateful look his way.

"We were out for a weekend of fishing and camping, and...ah...," Nathan told Conner, grinning, "I don't mind telling you, we're half-starved."

Brian pointed to his own chest with his thumb. "I'm all the way starved."

Conner laughed. "Nice to meet you, Brian." He shook the boy's hand. "Come on in. I've got some stew heating by the fire. It's simple food, but it'll fill your belly."

They went straight to the small wooden table that sat in one corner of the cabin. Nathan and Brian set down their packs and pulled out chairs for themselves while Conner went to fetch the pot from where it hung by the hearth.

"I don't have any bread to offer you. And there's nothing to drink here except water, but it's clean and cold."

Nathan waved away the apology in his cousin's voice. "We're just glad you're willing to share your breakfast with us. We have a long walk home and this will give us the energy to make the trip."

Brian sniffed the steam coming from the bowl that was set before him and then cocked an eyebrow at Nathan. Remembering how the teen reacted over the idea of snaring a rabbit yesterday, Nathan shook his head and said, "Don't ask. Just eat."

After one tentative taste, Brian gave an approving nod and dug in with relish. There was no talk as they satiated their hunger.

Afterward, Brian asked if he could go skip rocks on the lake until Nathan was ready to hike back to the rez. Nathan told him not to go too far off.

"Thanks for the food, Conner," the boy said.

"You're welcome."

Conner offered Brian a smile, but Nathan could see it didn't reach the man's eyes. As soon as Gwen's brother disappeared out the door, Nathan asked his cousin, "I'm sorry if we intruded on your solitude. But we really did need something to eat." This was met with silence. "So how are you doing?"

A dark cloud seemed to descend on Conner and the man just looked away.

Nathan felt compelled to say, "You've got to break free of this guilt, Conner. It's not doing anyone any good."

The man's whole body grew taut. "I don't want to talk about it."

An awkward silence fell between them.

Finally Conner asked, "Who's the boy?"

"He's the brother of a friend," Nathan told him. "Her name is Gwen and she's also Charity's teacher. We've exchanged kids for the weekend. She was to give my bruiser of a daughter some lessons in femininity. And I hoped to show Brian a little self-reliance." He barked out a humorless laugh. "I had to beg a meal to feed him. I sure hope Gwen's having better luck than I am."

Their dinner bowls scraped across the rough table-top as Conner gathered them up.

"Remember how Grandfather used to take us out?" he asked. "Just like you're taking Brian? Those times we had alone with him were special to us all, don't you think?"

"Yes." Nathan had many wonderful memories of hunting and tracking with Joseph. "Now *he* had survival skills! And he could weave a tale like no one else could. Still does, in fact."

"It was through those stories of his that he taught us all about life," Conner said. "He instilled integrity and honor in us. Taught us to be moral and upright. With words."

Both men fell silent, each lost in his own thoughts.

When the revelation came to Nathan, it was like a bolt from the sky. Maybe his shaman grandfather could help him encourage those same principles in Gwen's brother. The Great One certainly knew that Nathan had failed miserably this weekend. However, the idea of procuring Joseph's help with Brian had him sitting a little straighter. Hope had a way of doing that to a man.

"Listen," he said to his cousin, "I've got to be getting back to the rez. Gwen and Charity are expecting us before nightfall and it's going to be quite a hike." He rose from the chair. "Thanks for the meal."

"Anytime. You know that."

Nathan took a moment to study his cousin's face. If he could somehow ease Conner's burden, he would. But his problem was a big one. One that had to be faced alone. But he did say, "Grandfather would love to see you."

Conner's gaze narrowed. "Does he know I'm here?"

Lifting one shoulder a fraction, Nathan said, "I haven't said a word. And I don't plan to. But there's not much that Joseph Thunder doesn't know."

Sighing, his cousin just stared at a far corner of the room. "I'm not ready."

Nathan picked up both his pack and Brian's, then paused. "We're here for you. I want you to know that. If you need us, all you have to do is call and we'll come running."

"I know." But his cousin refused to meet his gaze.

The sun had been on its way to setting when Nathan and Brian made it home.

Gwen handed Nathan a tall glass of iced tea, and he thanked her with a tired smile. Charity had followed Brian to the back porch where the boy un-packed his knapsack.

Nathan wasn't the only one who was tired. Gwen was pooped. The two days she'd spent with Charity had been long and frustrating.

"You're not the only one who failed," she said after hearing him tell of the fiasco of a weekend he'd had with Brian.

"I'd planned a proper tea party," Gwen continued, "and somehow we ended up eating franks and beans. I was excited about teaching her how to braid her hair, and before I knew it, she'd talked me into learning the rules of soccer, instead. I got all the materials together to show her how to sew a simple bean-bag—" Gwen shook her head in wonder "—and Charity convinced me to watch stock-car racing on TV. And I bought the ingredients to make cookies, and we ended up outside making mud pies." The laughter that bubbled up from her throat couldn't be suppressed. "Pies made of wet, oozing mud, can you believe it?"

She lifted her gaze to Nathan's, the fondness she felt for his daughter gleaming in her eyes. "All my well-laid plans may have fallen flat, but I *have* learned one thing."

Nathan's brows rose in silent inquiry.

"That daughter of yours sure is an imp." Gwen's grin widened. "And when she turns on the charm, she's irresistible."

He wanted to agree, Gwen could tell, but dejection had him sighing heavily, instead.

"So was all this a waste of time for us?" he asked softly.

Wanting desperately to offer this man something positive after all he'd done for her and Brian, Gwen said, "I know it probably isn't much consolation, but Charity did talk a little about missing her mother." She chuckled, hoping to lift Nathan's pensive mood. "Amid all the mudslinging we did while playing her game of chef—"

"She talked about Ellen?" Nathan cut her off, his gaze one of interested surprise. "She hasn't mentioned her mother to me in all the weeks she's been with me."

Gwen paused a moment, then offered, "It seems she doesn't want to upset you. She has this notion that you and she might not be together if she upsets you. That—"

"Daddies don't stay."

The sound of his rusty whisper sent shivers coursing along her spine. "That's exactly what she said," Gwen told him.

"Charity said it to me, too."

"This idea she has about you leaving her," she said, "is also, I think, why she got so upset when you shouted in the teachers' lounge. She didn't seem too disturbed about being in trouble until you raised your voice. If you remember, that's when her eyes welled with tears and she looked about to cry. She said today that when daddies get mad, they leave."

Nathan nodded, his mind evidently churning.

Finally he said, "I'll control my temper. I don't

want my daughter feeling insecure. I want her to trust that I'll be here for her. Always."

He smiled, gratitude evident in every plane and angle of his handsome face. Gwen's heart pattered a quick beat.

"I guess you didn't completely fail with Charity," he whispered. "Thanks."

She wanted to speak, but overwhelming emotion stole away her words. Joy rushed through her at the thought that she may have helped him in some small way.

"Brian talked a little, too," he said.

Gwen's chin tipped up, her gaze latching on to his.

"Oh, he didn't disclose a whole lot," Nathan continued. "But he did wonder what he might have done to deserve the bad things that had happened to him in his life."

The happiness that had surged through her just a moment before was swamped by the thoughts of her brother's pain. Her shoulders slumped.

"I told him that we are often subjected to events and happenings that we have no control over, that we don't deserve." He looked away, then found her eyes on his once again. "It was a short conversation at best. And I did what I could to explain that he wasn't to blame. But the bitterness he expressed was…well, huge."

Gwen's surprise was huge, too. "Nathan, my brother has been to several counselors. Not one of them has been able to get him to open up about what happened to him."

"Now, I don't know that Brian was talking about the abuse he suffered—"

"Of course he was. What other 'bad things' could he have been referring to?"

Nathan nodded in agreement.

"This is wonderful," she said, sliding her hand over his forearm.

"It wasn't much—"

"It was *some*thing." Hope sprouted wings in her chest and soared.

He turned to her then, his sexy half grin making her feel wobbly-kneed weak.

"Yes, I guess it *was* something," he said, some emotion coating his voice with warmth. "Maybe this weekend wasn't as much of a loss as we both thought."

Their gazes locked, and the molecules in the air churned as the temperature seemed to rise several degrees. Gwen studied his intense cocoa-dark eyes, and a fire sparked in her soul, tiny flames licking at her from somewhere deep within, some needful place.

Then she saw it. The same powerful passion walloping her seemed to reverberate in waves from his entire being. Time slowed, and Gwen felt breathless as she waited for something to happen—for something was surely about to happen.

At the same instant, they leaned toward each other. The kiss they shared was chaste. Soul-stirringly sweet. It was a demonstration of the colossal gratefulness they both felt toward the other. She read the appreciation shining in his gaze when he pulled back and knew instinctively that her expression mirrored the same emotion.

But there was something else gurgling and simmering inside her. Something else reflecting in Nathan's expression. And that something was a desire so deep that it refused to be ignored.

The yearning building in them both seemed to swell, crowding out all other emotion. Once again, a powerful energy seemed to tug at them, and this time, Gwen knew there would be nothing soft and sweet about the meeting of their mouths.

Scorching heat. Luscious. Succulent. His kiss was ravaging, and just what she craved. He found her breast with his palm, encircling it gently, lovingly, and she reveled in the sparks his touch set off in her body.

The sound of ragged breathing filled her ears, and Gwen couldn't tell if it was his or her own. She didn't really care. All she wanted was his mouth on her, his hands on her. A small groan shimmied up from deep in her throat and she did nothing to quell it.

She wanted this. Desperately.

Combing her fingers through his dark hair, she opened her mouth to him, inviting him to deepen the intimacy between them. And it was an invitation he didn't hesitate to accept.

Had this kiss lasted seconds? Minutes? Hours? Gwen was so caught up in the passion slogging through her being that she lost track of time.

Finally he eased back. Not enough to break contact

with her, only enough to whisper raggedly against her lips, "Should we be doing this?"

"Probably not." The words were spoken before she'd even had time to think. "But I don't care."

His breathy chuckle was hot against her skin, his lips so close to hers that she actually felt a tickle.

"Me, neither," he murmured.

He covered her mouth with his once more, and the two of them seemed to draw closer, if that was possible.

At that moment, an errant thought sighed through her mind: *We could be one.*

One. Oh, how she'd love to be one with this man! One mind. One body. One soul.

The mere idea had her heart racing even faster. If she followed whim and desire, she'd rip off her clothes right here and now. She'd tug and pull at his shirt until he came free of it.

But somewhere from the back of her brain came a warning that there were children in the house. Charity. And Brian.

Getting naked in her living room was totally out of the question. No matter how much the idea appealed to her.

Gwen forced herself to splay her palm against Nathan's broad chest. Even with this new determination to subdue the desire raging inside her, she was fully aware of his sinewy pectoral muscles. But she pushed at him, backed away several inches before the ravenous miasma could discombobulate her again.

"We can't do this." As she spoke, she slipped off

the couch and moved around to stand behind him. Disappointment fairly pulsed from him. "Here," she offered in consolation, "let me do something nice for you, instead."

She began kneading his shoulders and the stiff muscles of his neck. The heat of him penetrated his cotton shirt. The bare skin of his neck seared her fingertips, and her blood heated until she wondered if giving him a massage was such a good idea, after all. With longing thrumming through her, she continued to rub. But rather than relax him, her ministrations only seemed to make him tenser.

Finally he reached up and clasped both her wrists, quelling the movement of her hands.

He tilted his head to the side, his dark, dark eyes finding hers. The emotion roiling in his gaze was so intense that it stole her breath away. She felt encapsulated in a sweltering void.

Nathan drew her down until their mouths were a mere breath apart.

If he didn't kiss her, if she didn't feel his lips on hers, Gwen was certain she'd lose her sanity.

He continued to tug, and she knew suddenly that he didn't mean to stop until he'd pulled her over the back of the sofa and into his lap. She let herself roll over top the cushioned couch back, and she couldn't help but chuckle sensuously at this risqué behavior in which the two of them were engaged.

She whispered his name with sexy censure, but the rusty quality of her voice only seemed to incite him further. He growled her name, and she thought she'd die from the need to feel his hands on her.

His passion was clearly evident as the length of him pressed against her backside, rock hard, and at that moment she did wish that the two of them were stretched out on her bed, behind closed doors.

But they were not. And that was the cold, cruel reality of the moment.

The sound of voices and footfalls on the kitchen floor had both Nathan and Gwen blinking their way out of the hungry fog clutching at them. The children were coming. They pulled apart, frustration splashing over them like a dash of frigid water, a nearly tangible thing.

Their passion would have to wait, and Gwen forced herself to slide off his lap in order to cement that idea into her reluctant mind. She straightened her clothes, smoothed her fingers over her hair. She was astonished at how quickly her feelings for this man had developed and grown into something deep. A connection that sprang from the very essence of her.

He was a good man. She'd learned that. He was a trustworthy man. And there seemed to be so few of those in the world. She decided there and then that Nathan was a treasure. A treasure she wanted for her own.

Chapter Six

All was quiet at Smoke Valley. All, that is, except for the one bar that was located on a side street just off the main road cutting straight through the rez. Nathan heard the muffled music blaring as he drove by the drinking establishment. He glanced at his watch. The business would close in about thirty minutes, and then the rest of his late-night shift would prove uneventful, he was sure.

One of the problems in the police department recently was the fact that there was only one officer on duty during the night shift. Nathan didn't think that was safe, no matter how peaceful the rez seemed. So he'd come up with the swing schedule that necessitated each one of his officers taking an evening shift one night every two weeks to supplement the regular third-shift officers. The men and women working for him didn't seem to like the idea much, but when he presented the schedule and they saw that he was willing to take his turn in the rotation, they more readily accepted the change.

On Nathan's night shifts, he asked his grandfather to come to his house to stay with Charity. He wanted her to sleep in her own bed so that her routine wouldn't be broken and she'd be well rested for school.

He was just reaching to call in to the dispatcher his intention of taking a quick break for a cup of coffee when his radio crackled.

"Nathan, you there?"

A quick flash of irritation had him issuing a sigh. He'd been attempting to get all three of his dispatchers to learn the formal police system of numbered codes used to make communicating by radio clear, concise and more efficient. However, something in the man's tone told Nathan not to argue the point at this time.

"I'm here," he said.

"George from the Rusty Nail just called in."

Stress. That was what he heard in the dispatcher's voice. Nathan knew that George was the owner of the bar.

"Trouble?" Nathan asked.

"Yeah. A fight. Sounds like a bad one, too. Want me to make some calls? Get some extra help in here?"

"Let me check it out first. I'm on my way." Then he pressed the button on the mike once more. "Walt," he called to the other officer on patrol for the night, "if you can hear me, get yourself over to the Rusty Nail."

The surge of adrenaline pumping through Nathan's veins heightened his awareness, quickened his responses. He made a precise three-point turn, the thought of a coffee break forgotten as he flipped on his lights and siren and headed back toward the bar.

When Nathan pushed his way into the dim and smoky confines of the building, the tension in the air was so crisp and the patrons so quiet, it would have been impossible not to realize that something ominous was going down. Heads swiveled in his direction when the door shut behind him.

He assessed the situation in an instant. Two groups of young men were facing off. He knew most of the men in the larger group, and every single one of them looked not only ready but anxious for a brawl. The smaller group was made up of males who were strangers to him. One of them wielded a knife, the long blade reflecting the red and blue neon lights of the various liquor signs gracing the walls. The craggy-faced owner of the establishment, George, stood at one end of the bar gripping a wooden baseball bat.

"Put that thing down," was Nathan's first order.

Rather than obey, George just narrowed his eyes.

There was ice in Nathan's tone when he said, "Did you hear me?"

George tucked the bat behind the bar, but it was clear he didn't like having to do it.

Nathan knew from previous experience that the first order of business was to gain control over the situation. The crowd was angry, most of them inebriated. If Nathan failed to prove to them—quickly—that he was the one in charge, then the trouble lurking around the edges would come rushing at them all, full force.

"I don't know what's going on," Nathan said to everyone in the room, "and I don't care. All I do know is that you're going to break this up. Now. And you're all going to leave peacefully."

He directed his gaze to the man holding the weapon. "Put the knife down on the bar and back away from it."

The authority in his tone already had several of the men inching away from the core of disruption. But the man who was the focus of Nathan's attention evidently had no intention of doing what he was told. His chin jutted forward obstinately.

"And give these guys a chance to jump me?" he asked. "No way, man. No way I'm giving up my knife."

"We can do this easy—" as he spoke, Nathan crept stealthily forward "—or we can do this hard."

The perpetrator had sealed his fate by refusing to comply with Nathan's command. The man was bound for jail. Easy or hard. His arrest was going to happen.

There was a soft but almost collective gasp when the man suddenly turned the knife on Nathan. He wobbled, the excessive alcohol in his system dimming his reflexes and his common sense.

"Come on," the man taunted. "You feelin' lucky?"

Instinctively Nathan lowered his center of gravity. He'd had extensive training in subduing a belligerent and dangerous drunk. Waiting for the opportunity and then acting swiftly were the two most important tasks at hand.

Out of the blue, Nathan was swallowed up by thoughts of his daughter. What would Charity do if he was killed by this drunken idiot? She had no one. She'd be left utterly alone.

Then the image of Gwen's gorgeous green eyes floated through his mind. If he died tonight, would she mourn him?

Unbidden visions of his fallen comrades' widows, their faces red, their eyes puffy from weeping, swam into his brain. He blinked as emotion swirled and churned.

With a silent but vicious expletive, he thrust the worrisome pictures from his mind. All of them. His only thought should be the here and now. Disarming this hooligan should be his sole focus.

An opportunity to attack came when Walt, his fellow officer, entered the bar. The perp's attention was averted for a split second, but that was all Nathan needed. He sprang at the man.

Luck, apparently, wasn't completely on his side. The man shifted swiftly, and Nathan felt a burning pain when the knife connected with his forearm. But Nathan's grasp became like iron. Hearing the clatter of the knife hitting the floor, he wrestled with the man only briefly before he overpowered him.

Walt was at his side, handcuffs at the ready. The

drunk was cursing as he lay on the filthy floorboards of the bar, Nathan's knee firmly on the small of his back.

"This is over," Nathan called out to the onlookers as he fastened the man's wrists together with the cuffs. "The bar is closed for the night. Go home. All of you." He looked over at Walt. "Thanks. You showed up just in time."

"Wish I'd arrived a few minutes sooner," the officer said.

Nathan shook his head. "You came in the door and grabbed his attention. Gave me the perfect chance to rush him."

Walt noticed the crimson stain on his boss's sleeve. "You're hurt. Let me take him in and start the paperwork. You go get that looked at."

Certain that his arm would need stitches without even having looked at the wound, Nathan didn't refuse. "Thanks. I'll catch up with you later."

The cut was small, but deep. Nathan used a bar towel supplied by George to staunch the flow of blood. And the bar owner was nice enough to offer to drive Nathan to his brother's house. Nathan rang the bell and waited.

At last a bleary-eyed Grey opened the door.

"Ah, good." Nathan grinned. "The doctor's in."

His brother yawned. "You know what time it is? Some reason you think you don't have to make an appointment like everyone else?"

Like Nathan, Grey had only recently returned to Smoke Valley, after a stint of college and medical school, and a couple of years spent practicing medicine with his wife. But the marriage had soured, and Grey had returned to the rez a divorced man. The breakup had affected his brother mightily. Nathan sensed it, even though Grey had thus far refused to talk about what he'd gone through.

Grey's gaze darted to the bloodstain on Nathan's shirtsleeve. Concern puckered his brow. "Why didn't you say you were hurt?" Grey stepped back, ushering Nathan inside. "I'll grab my keys and we'll run over to the office. What happened?"

Nathan filled him in as they walked next door to the office. When they arrived, Grey flipped on the bright overhead lights in one examining room. "Hop up there on the table and let me have a look at you." He gathered antiseptic and gauze.

Once Nathan had tugged off his shirt, slowly peeling the cloth from his wounded forearm, his brother whistled.

"Going to need at least a couple of stitches." Grey turned back to the cabinet for more supplies.

Nathan gritted his teeth as the cut was cleaned, and he felt the urge to compliment his brother on how swiftly and painlessly Grey managed to numb the wound area with a shot of novocaine.

"I'm getting pretty good at giving needles," Grey commented. "It was common practice in med school to allow the nurses to do the prep work, but when one isn't available…"

"You still haven't found a nurse?"

His brother shook his head as he touched Nathan's

arm near the cut to test for numbness. "I'm getting desperate. My practice is growing. I even have patients coming in from Mountview. I need some help."

"You have residents of Mountview coming onto the rez to see you?"

Grey chuckled. "Don't sound so shocked. I'm a good doctor."

"I wasn't suggesting you weren't. But you've got to admit that it's strange."

"Yes. I admit that. There are perfectly good doctors practicing in the town of Mountview."

His brother's jaw went rigid, and Nathan got the clear message that it would be best to let this touchy subject drop.

The two were quiet as Grey worked to stitch Nathan's skin back together. As he watched the needle being pushed through one side of the cut and out the other, Nathan felt himself fill with a chilly anxiety. He could so easily have lost his life. With each suture that was tied, his icy fear grew.

"And to think," he murmured softly, "I brought Charity to Smoke Valley because I thought it would be safer here. For both of us."

Taking this job as sheriff was supposed to ensure that he'd be around to take care of his daughter. But tonight had brought him to the terrible conclusion that he was no more out of harm's way on the rez than he would be anywhere else.

Gwen's beautiful face flashed through his thoughts and sweat broke out across his brow.

"You okay?" his brother asked. "Can you feel the stitches?"

"I'm fine."

That was one of the biggest, bold-faced lies Nathan had ever told. He was anything but fine. He was sick. At heart.

While working in New York City, he'd steered clear of getting himself involved with women. However, since moving to Vermont he'd relaxed his guard. He'd thought it safe to allow his emotions a little freedom. But he now realized that coming to care for Gwen had been a mistake.

His eyes closed, and the scene that swam behind his lids shook him to the core. He saw Gwen's wan face shrouded in a black veil. He heard her sobs. Saw her eyes swollen with tears.

The snip of the scissors returned him to the here and now.

"All set," Grey said. "In a week or so you'll be right as rain."

"Good. Thanks."

His brother's head tilted a fraction. "You sure you're okay?"

He was now. He really was. So he nodded.

Grey suggested he go right home and rest, but Nathan had something he had to do before following the doctor's orders.

His mind felt as numb as his forearm as he drove through the now-tranquil night. He pulled up outside the station house, parked and got out of the car. As though he was walking in some sort of trance, he went inside. Nodding silently at the dispatcher, he answered no questions. Only made straight for his office.

He closed the door behind him, then fished in his pocket.

The penny looked dull as it sat in the palm of his hand. Opening the lid of the large jar of coins, he dropped it in.

He hadn't felt compelled to add to his jar of luck since moving to the rez. But tonight had changed all that. Tonight had taught him that danger lurked everywhere. Even in what seemed to be the safest of places—the rez. He promised himself to go back to adding pennies to the jar every day he returned to the office. Maybe that way, he'd be less likely to lower his guard again.

It was going to crush him to do the right thing. But the right thing was the *only* thing he could do if he was going to be able to sleep nights.

Putting some distance between himself and Gwen was the right thing.

For Gwen's sake.

The clock must be broken. That was all there was to it. There was no other explanation for the way the hands had moved so slowly over the course of the day.

For what felt like the thousandth time, Gwen darted a glance at the big numbers centered up there on the wall above the blackboard. How on earth could time move so slowly?

It was Gwen's habit to ask her students to share any news with their classmates. Most mornings she'd form the information into simple sentences that the class would use to practice their printing. However, this morning Charity's news had almost floored Gwen.

The child stood up and announced to everyone that her dad had been stabbed while he'd been on duty the night before. Sudden fear shot through Gwen. As gently as possible, she asked Charity if her father was all right. The child said he was, but Gwen wanted to see Nathan with her own eyes.

The school day had dragged.

Gwen had plenty of time to come to understand just how much this stoic and proud man had come to mean to her. She'd lost her heart to him, that much was clear to her. He'd made it possible for her to trust again. And for that she was grateful. But what she felt for him was more than mere gratitude. Nathan had showed that he cared. For her. For her brother.

In a hundred different ways, he'd displayed his intention of sharing—sometimes even lifting—the burdens she carried. He was kind. And he listened. Gwen couldn't remember the last time she'd had someone really listen to and show an interest in what she had to say or how she felt.

And now she'd discovered that the man she'd fallen in love with had been hurt. Stabbed with a knife.

Anxiety gnawed at her.

Another darted glance at the clock. It was broken. The contraption had to be broken!

But finally the school secretary's voice came over the public-address system as she made the afternoon announcements. And then the children were released for the day.

"Charity, honey," Gwen said, "come here."

"Yes?"

"Do you know if your dad's at home?" she asked.

"I don't think so. He said he was gonna sleep for a little while and then go back to work." Charity fidgeted, obviously anxious to get out of the classroom. "Granddad is picking me up. In fact, he's prolly waiting for me."

Instinct had Gwen saying, "Probably." Then she added, "Okay, you go on. Don't keep your grandfather waiting."

Once the room was empty, Gwen straightened her desk quickly, packed her attaché case with papers that needed grading and then she headed out the door. But rather than walk in the direction of her small house, she turned and made for the police department.

Yes, she could call him, but Nathan would surely pooh-pooh her concern. She wouldn't be satisfied that he was truly okay until she saw him with her own eyes. Felt him under her own fingertips.

She pushed her way through the door and asked the man at the desk if Sheriff Thunder was available.

"Sure," the dispatcher said, but then a call came over the radio and the phone rang simultaneously, so he jerked a thumb in the direction she should go.

Gwen hurried down the short hallway and knocked on the office door.

"Come in."

Just hearing Nathan's voice sounding so strong made relief wash through her being. She walked in and smiled hello.

His features expressed alarm as he stood by the file cabinet. "Is Charity okay?"

"She's fine," Gwen rushed to assure him. "I'm here about you." She inched closer even though she was overtaken by a bout of self-consciousness. "Charity said you were hurt last night. 'Stabbed' was the word she used." A tremor forced her to pause. Her chin dipped almost of its own volition and she found herself looking up at him through half-raised lashes. She swallowed, her throat painful with the magnitude of emotion she felt. She whispered, "I've been scared to death all day long, Nathan. I came because I needed to see for myself that you're okay."

Sexual tension hummed in the air between them. Gwen wanted desperately to rush at him and feel the solidness of him beneath her fingertips. To press her mouth to his. To show him how much she cared. To discover that he really and truly was alive and unharmed.

However, slowly and inexplicably, the air changed. Almost as if a crisp breeze had blown in through the window, the magnetism that had plucked and pulled at them both metamorphosed into something else. Something new. Something that chilled to the point of discomfort.

Nathan's intense gaze took on a distinct standoff-ishness that had Gwen frowning with bewilderment.

"I appreciate your concern."

Although his proclamation was spoken softly, the formality in his tone was like a punch to the solar plexus. Blindsided, Gwen fought to remain standing there as if all was well and normal.

What she wanted to do was press both hands to her gut. To open her mouth wide with the shock roiling through her. But she simply stood there.

He didn't seem the least bit distressed that she'd worried about him all day long. That she'd spent hours fretting over his safety.

The apathy he displayed was enough to steal her breath away.

Finally she could remain silent no longer. "What's wrong, Nathan?"

Immediately his gaze dropped to the forms he held in his hands.

"Nothing's wrong." He perused the papers. "Why should anything be wrong?"

Without waiting for her to answer, he rounded his desk and sat down.

"I've got a lot of work to do, Gwen. We made an arrest last night and I have paperwork waiting."

Gwen felt disoriented. Completely confused by his cool behavior. It was clear that he was suggesting she take her leave, but she couldn't do that. Not just yet.

"Nathan," she said, taking another step into his office, "I...I care about you. I thought...I thought we were f-friends."

Her tongue tripped over the word and Gwen knew why. She didn't like the description. It wasn't accurate. She'd thought they were well on their way to being much more than friends.

His dark gaze leveled on her then. Intense. Concentrated.

"We *are* friends."

Gwen went utterly still. He was sending a message with that small statement. A clear, unmistakable message.

Friends. That was all they were. And that was all they'd ever be. For her to expect more than that was a mistake.

"But I just…" The rest of her thought petered out, her mind was in that much turmoil.

He'd kissed her. He'd desired her. She'd seen it. Felt it.

Hadn't she?

"Look," he said, his tone firmer now, "I'm okay. I was involved in a little scuffle last night. Got myself cut. But I'm all stitched up and I'm going to be just fine." He picked up a manila file folder and stuffed the papers into it. "When you're in my line of work, you have to expect this kind of thing."

Still, she couldn't move. Couldn't even breathe.

His gaze flattened and his mouth drew down at the corners. "Gwen, it seems clear that…well, that you thought…that you were mistaken about…some things."

"Mistaken?"

Had that weak utterance really been voiced by her?

He sighed. "I don't want to do this. As I said, I appreciate your concern. Now, if you'll excuse me..."

It was a dismissal. *Another* dismissal.

This one she heeded.

As she walked out of the station house, Gwen felt almost disembodied. As if she were floating. The *click-click* of her heels on the pavement was the only evidence that she was actually walking away.

Gwen wasn't just hurt by Nathan's unanticipated, chilly reserve. She felt devastated.

She'd given more of herself to him than she had to any other man—not only her trust, but her heart. And he'd turned a cold cheek to her.

This kind of behavior was familiar to Gwen. She'd seen it before. She'd seen it exhibited first by her father, then by her stepfather.

She'd thought Nathan was different from the other men in her life. Men who acted caring and giving one moment, cold and distant the next. Men who ruled their environment by oppressing and controlling those around them.

Yes, she'd thought Nathan was unique. That he was distinctly different. But she'd learned today that he was just like all the others.

Just like them.

Chapter Seven

Her blazing curls pooled around her shoulders as she leaned her weight on one elbow, her attention focused on something on her desktop. Nathan had missed seeing her the past few days, had missed the sound of her voice. However, missing her hadn't been what had brought him to see her.

His conscience had.

Standing here staring at her wasn't going to get this chore over and done with. Wanting to let her know she wasn't alone, he shifted from one foot to the other and cleared his throat.

She wasn't expecting anyone. That much he read from the surprise in her expression. But the instant she saw who had come to see her, her green gaze clouded with hurt and something else—something that cut him to the quick.

Wariness.

Well, why shouldn't she guard herself? Hadn't he treated her abominably? Hadn't he been callous and thoughtless of her feelings? She had every right to want to shield herself from the likes of him.

"Nathan."

Her greeting wasn't cold, exactly. He had the fleeting thought that he'd somehow have felt better if it had been. At least then he'd know that she still felt *something*.

Hell, man, his brain railed silently, *you have no right to that*. It was true. Their situation hadn't changed. It wasn't as if he was here to start anything up with her. No, he'd only come to explain. She deserved that much. But the fact that her eyes had been so wary when she'd first seen him and her greeting sounded indifferent…well, he'd be lying if he said that didn't bother him.

You have no right to feel bothered by anything she chooses to do, his inner voice accused. Again he had to concede.

"Gwen." He nodded and took a tentative step forward. "You busy?"

Glancing down at her desk and then back at him, she said, "Actually I am. I'm late with my monthly teacher's plan. Mrs. Halley's expecting it before I leave for the day."

"Then I won't keep you." But rather than making himself scarce as she was plainly suggesting, he continued to inch his way into the classroom. "I came to talk to you."

"About Charity?"

"No. About..." He couldn't get himself to say *us,* so he just let that thought fade. Then he tried again. "About what happened the last time I saw you...about my behavior in my office when you came by to see me the day after I got hurt while on duty."

He was talking too much. Nathan was certain she remembered their last meeting. The hurt he'd known she felt would have been hard for her to forget, yet here he was detailing the moment as if it had taken place years ago, rather than days ago.

She put down her pen. Curiosity had her brow puckering, but her gaze never lost one iota of heedfulness. It was clear to Nathan that she didn't intend to allow him to catch her unawares a second time.

Living with the fact that he'd wounded her was bad enough, but he hated the thought that he was the cause of this new cautiousness she displayed.

She rested her chin on her fist. "I'm listening."

The fact that she hadn't invited him in, that she hadn't encouraged him to make himself comfortable, wasn't lost on him. She wanted him gone as quickly as possible. That was more than obvious.

"First off," he said, "I want to apologize."

Her green eyes were cool, and as deep as Smoke Lake in the early spring. Her beautiful face seemed void of emotion.

He sighed. "When you came to see me, you were concerned for me, for my safety. I disregarded your feelings. I want you to know that I was...wrestling with some things. I'd like to explain those things. To try to help you…understand why I was…why I acted the way I did.''

Her expression didn't change. This was harder than he'd imagined it was going to be.

Guilt had poked and prodded and needled him. It had occupied his mind while he was in the office by day and kept him from sleeping soundly at night. He hoped rationalizing his behavior to her, apologizing for having disregarded her concern for him, would put all that to rest. Nathan felt compelled to press forward even though, from all the outward signs she expressed, she didn't seem to care one way or the other.

"You see," he continued, "while I was working as a cop in New York City, I was very careful not to allow myself to…get involved with anyone. I kept a strict distance between myself and…well, any women I might meet.

"Law enforcement is a dangerous profession. I've attended more than one funeral where I watched wives and children sob out their grief over the coffins of their husbands and fathers who had been killed in the line of duty.''

Gwen didn't look disinterested any longer. She sat up straight, her hands in her lap now, her gaze lighting with a pensive intensity while she listened in attentive silence.

"When Charity entered my life," he went on, "I was scared to death. Scared that something would happen to me and I would end up leaving her all alone. So I came home. I moved back to the rez thinking that I was safer here. That I could cheat death by working in what I'd thought was a peaceful place.''

He swallowed, shifted his weight. No man liked to admit he was wrong, that he'd come to an erroneous conclusion.

''I relaxed my guard, Gwen.'' He forced himself to level his gaze on hers. He needed her to understand just how sorry he was that he'd allowed a relationship to develop between them. ''I allowed myself to believe I was safe. I allowed myself to…well, to become too friendly. With you.

''I learned really quickly that what I do for a living is dangerous no matter where I do it. I'm often forced to face off with people who want to do me harm. Some evil person with a gun—or a knife—could cause my death. Anyplace. Anytime. One slipup and I could find myself meeting the Great Spirit. It just isn't fair for me to expect someone—a girlfriend, a wife—to live with the fear that I might not come home from work one day.''

Her eyes took on a softness that affected Nathan deeply, provoked him to avert his gaze for a moment.

''Our friendship was growing,'' he forced himself to continue. ''My feelings for you…''

He paused. He hadn't meant to delve into this most sensitive area. She didn't need to understand what he might or might not have been feeling for her. She simply needed to appreciate his reasons for wanting to put some distance between them.

''I need you to understand why I can't allow myself

to become involved," he finally finished. "You deserve that much."

What he wanted to tell her was that he believed she deserved more from a relationship than suffering the daily fear over his safety. Well, he guessed that was exactly what he was telling her...even if it was in a roundabout way.

"I want you to know that I—" His jaw snapped shut. He couldn't get his tongue to utter the word *love*. "I liked being with you, Gwen. I liked that you and my daughter seemed to get along so well. I liked interacting with Brian. You need to know that my breaking things off between us," he continued, "is about me. It's my fault." He averted his gaze. Why did he feel so desolate inside?

"Well—" he heaved a sigh "—I came here to apologize. And to explain. I've done that." He gave the door a darting glance. "I guess I'll go."

Gwen remained silent and still, letting her emotions ebb like a vast and empty ocean as she watched him turn on his heel and walk out of her classroom.

The first emotion that surfaced was sadness, and that surprised her. She'd been very hurt the last time she'd seen Nathan. He'd acted so cold, as if she was nothing special to him. As if she was some kind of nonentity.

When she'd looked up and seen him standing in the doorway a few moments ago, she'd expected fury to blaze in her like a bonfire. However, she'd been able to show no emotion at all. Her childhood had made her adept at blanking all feeling from her expression. Even when her insides were roiling with fear or humiliation, anxiety or panic, she could don a vacant mask. Often, that had been her only chance of emotional survival when it came to her father and her stepfather.

The sorrow in her chest welled like a wave and she let it surge through her entire being.

It was a shame that Nathan had spent his life avoiding intimate relationships because he feared his occupation would leave his significant other bereft. Understanding his feelings was pretty easy after hearing him explain his fear. The idea of leaving behind grieving family and friends could be an overwhelming burden. For anyone. And it seemed that, for Nathan, it was weight he'd decided not to carry.

Then another—peculiar—emotion rose up in her. Relief.

The fact that Nathan had acted so pitilessly had led her to believe he was just like the other men she'd grown up around. Men who emotionally tormented and broke down those they supposedly loved by acting affectionate one moment and then doing a complete about-face the next. Men whose actions and deeds were based on nothing more than meanspiritedness and the need to control.

But Nathan wasn't like her father and stepfather. Not at all.

His behavior toward her in his office had been caused by his fear. He'd been wounded on the job, and he was just coming to grips with the fact that he wasn't as safe here at Smoke Valley Reservation as he had thought.

No wonder he'd been sharp with her. No wonder he'd been distant.

Then a thought flitted through her mind. Nathan must be worried sick. This incident had rekindled his anxiety about dying. And although he could distance himself from Gwen and Brian, he couldn't do the same with Charity. She was his daughter. She was a responsibility from which he couldn't separate himself.

How, she wondered, would he reconcile himself with that?

Saying that she was disheartened about Nathan's desire to ignore the attraction that had sparked between them would certainly be putting it mildly. She'd come to the conclusion that he was the kind of man to whom she wouldn't mind losing her heart.

Who was she kidding? Nathan had already stolen her heart *and* her soul. However, he did have solid motivation for his actions.

She was an adult. A mournful sigh issued forth from her throat almost of its own volition. She was just going to have to learn to live with Nathan's decision.

The front door opened and closed. Brian was home. Gwen stood at the sink washing up a few dishes. She expected to hear her brother's bedroom door slam shut, but he surprised her by entering the kitchen.

"Hey," he greeted her.

Gwen turned and smiled at him over her shoulder. For a second, she resumed washing the glass that was in her hand, but the sight of Brian's grinning face had her twisting back around to face him.

"That old shaman is amazing," he said.

Her mouth quirked up at one corner and she gently chastised, "I'm not sure Joseph Thunder would appreciate being called old. But he'd welcome being thought of as amazing."

So, the night of storytelling at Joseph's house had gone well. When Brian had come home full of excitement at having been invited by Nathan, Gwen had been pleasantly surprised. Actually she'd been astonished.

At first she'd allowed herself to fantasize that Nathan had changed his mind, that he was trying to rekindle their relationship though her brother. However, when Nathan did all the communicating about the evening through Brian, the obvious care he took in not calling or contacting her personally told Gwen that her fantasies were just that. Fantasies.

But her heart was touched by the fact that, although he'd called a halt to their personal relationship, Nathan was still doing what he could to help Brian. This invitation to the gathering the shaman was hosting was a way for Brian to learn more about Native American culture. Her brother would have contact with honorable role models. And he'd get the chance to meet other boys living on the reservation.

"So how many children came to the gathering?" she asked him, wiping the suds from her hands.

"Not too many," Brian told her. "There were six other boys my age. A few girls. And a handful of smaller kids. Charity was there. Did you know—" it had been years since Gwen had seen her brother's eyes dance with such excitement "—that a long time ago each tribe of Kolheeks was known as a clan? And that each clan was thought of as family, so a brave—that's a young male—couldn't choose a wife from his own clan? He had to go out to another clan to find someone to marry."

Gwen had read this while doing research on the Kolheeks, but not wanting to dampen Brian's fire, she simply responded, "That's interesting."

"And did you know," he continued in a flurry, "that boys my age were taken all the way around to the other side of the mountain—out in the middle of nowhere—and had to find their way back to the tribe? They had to provide their own food and shelter and everything. They could only take one tool with them. They had to choose from a bow and arrow, an ax or a knife. If they made it back, they were thought of as men. They were given the same respect, the same privileges."

He went to the refrigerator and poured himself a glass of juice. After taking a quick drink, he wiped his mouth with the back of his hand.

"All of us got into a big argument about what weapon would be the best to take."

Gwen couldn't help but ask, "Which would you choose?"

"I'd take the ax. A bow would do me no good."

He laughed. "Even if I had a whole quiver of arrows. And a knife isn't heavy enough to chop down trees. But an ax can cut firewood and chop down branches for shelter. If you needed to, you could even use it to whack some unsuspecting animal for food." He wrinkled his nose, adding, "I'd have to be awful hungry, though, to kill an animal for my dinner."

She chuckled.

"Just thinking about it makes me grateful for grocery stores," he said.

"I know exactly what you mean." Again she joined in with his laughter.

This exhilaration Brian was showing was a joy for Gwen to see. His evening with Joseph and the Kolheek children and teens was the cause. She owed Nathan a great debt for including her brother in the evening's events.

Brian's smile faded, his clear green eyes sobering, as he said, "I wish I was Kolheek. I wish I had been born and raised here. I like the things they believe. When we were out for the weekend, Nathan told me that every living being deserves respect." The boy went quiet for a moment. Then his gaze intensified. "He's right, Gwen."

The fact that her brother had come to an amazing realization wasn't lost on her. And he wasn't thinking about other living beings—he was thinking about himself. He was grasping the concept that *he* deserved to be respected. Years of his father's ill treatment had somehow led him to believe he wasn't worthy of consideration or regard. Nathan, through his actions and his deeds, had somehow changed Brian's thinking about himself.

"He *is* right," Gwen agreed. "There's no doubt in my mind."

Hefting the grocery bag higher on her hip, Gwen eyed the doorway of the police station as she walked up the block. How she'd love to go inside and talk to Nathan. Thank him for all he was doing for Brian.

But she'd go right on by. Nathan had made his desires known. He didn't want to be her friend. She meant to respect that.

Just as she came to the door, it opened and he stepped out onto the pavement. She had the odd thought that the moment couldn't have been more perfect had she choreographed it.

"Hello, Gwen."

Nathan removed his sunglasses and she met his gaze. Her heart hammered.

"Hi," she said.

The September afternoon seemed to heat up. They made a little small talk, the way casual acquaintances do, talking about the most mundane of things—the weather, the traffic, local happenings—but there was nothing casual about the attraction between them. It started slow, like a mist entwining itself amid their feet and legs. Then the magnetism rose and thickened, pulling and drawing higher and higher, until Gwen found it difficult to inhale.

Nathan felt it, too. That was obvious. The muscles

just beneath the sharp angles of his handsome face grew taut, almost hawklike.

Unable to quell her tongue, she blurted, "I am so grateful to you." Without waiting for him to respond, she told him all that Brian had revealed to her about his new way of thinking. Finally she said, "He's discovering that he's a valuable human being. That he didn't deserve the treatment he got from his father."

"I'm glad to hear that." Nathan slid his finger and thumb along the metal arm of his sunglasses. "It would be nearly impossible for Brian to grow into a self-confident young man as long as he thought his father was somehow justified in his actions."

Her smile was brilliant. "It was you, Nathan, and living on the rez and that wonderful grandfather of yours. If Brian and I hadn't come here..." She shook her head, reaching out and sliding her fingers over his forearm.

Gwen felt the zip and zing of something akin to an electrical current pass between them, and it was all she could do not to gasp in reaction. Raising her eyes to his, she saw that he'd gone utterly still, barely breathing.

The moment throbbed, quivered, like a balloon that had been overfilled with some thick, gelatinous material and was ready to burst.

Then he pulled away just far enough to free himself from her touch. Gwen was saddened to feel the enchantment seep away.

"How about dinner tonight?" She was as surprised by the question as he seemed to be.

"Gwen," he said, averting his gaze to the small space between their feet, "I don't think that's a good idea."

"As friends, Nathan," she stressed. "I want to thank you. For all you've done for Brian. And don't say you're not free. Brian said Joseph is having another meeting tonight, and I know Charity attends. Come on. It'll be fun."

Caution clouded his eyes. "As friends?"

She heard his tone and knew that he doubted that either one of them could follow though on the plan.

"You've made yourself perfectly clear about not wanting to be...involved," she told him. "I'm a big girl. I can handle this. If friendship is all we're going to have, then so be it." She glanced into the grocery bag she carried. "Besides, I have a steak in here with your name on it."

Seconds ticked by and still he hesitated. Then she sensed the tension in his body relax.

"A steak, huh?"

"Yes." She smiled. "And corn on the cob, mashed potatoes, sliced tomatoes and biscuits. Homemade."

When he smiled, she perceived that every bit of his apprehension had evaporated.

"Now who in their right mind could pass up homemade biscuits?"

Heat rushed through her, and Gwen could only describe the feeling as nothing short of pure bliss.

Chapter Eight

Liar, liar, pants on fire.

The childhood taunt raced repeatedly through Gwen's mind. She warned her young students about goading one another with such immature insults, but this one just seemed to stick in her brain like gummy white glue.

She'd assured Nathan earlier today that their dinner together was as friends. That her only intention was to thank him for being so good, so kind to her brother. When she'd said it, she'd meant it.

Hadn't she?

Oh, stop deluding yourself, a quiet but insistent voice mocked.

Okay, so she wanted him. No, it was more than mere want. She loved the man. And she knew in her heart that Nathan felt something for her, too. Something deep. Something real.

She read it in his dark gaze. Saw it in the ever-present tension of his handsome, falconlike features.

But the fact remained that no matter what emotions might be churning around inside him, he wasn't willing to follow his heart. He was a person whose will was clearly stronger than sentiment. His strength of character seemed to easily overpower the desires of his body.

"What a lucky man," she murmured, examining her reflection in the shiny chrome toaster sitting on the counter. She combed her fingers through her curls.

Gwen picked up the tray on which she'd placed two bottles of beer and two mugs that had spent the past couple of hours frosting in the freezer, and then she went out onto the small back porch where Nathan waited.

"Here we go." She'd offered him his choice of apple pie or a cold beer after their meal. Apparently, tonight his thirst took precedence over his sweet tooth.

"Thanks again, Gwen," he said, satisfaction in his tone as he absently rubbed his flattened palm over his abdomen. "Dinner was delicious."

She accepted the compliment with a smile as she opened first one beer, then the other, and poured them into the mugs. She handed one to him.

Their eyes met. Desire hummed almost audibly. She could sense it. Feel it. And she knew beyond a shadow of a doubt that he could, too.

The craving that tempted them had been there since he'd arrived. Not to mention all through dinner. However, Gwen had decided that if Nathan was determined to ignore it, then she could darn well do the same.

She sat down in the creaky old rocker and took a sip of the yeasty foam.

"It's so quiet here," she said, stopping long enough to lick traces of froth from her upper lip. "I've come to love the quiet."

A stillness settled over them. A tranquil silence. She felt so serene being with him here tonight that she felt she could say anything and it would be okay. So...she did.

"You know," she began, "I like knowing that you're willing to really live your convictions."

His dark gaze took on a guardedness.

"I'm serious," she assured him, hoping to convey that she had no hidden agenda with the opinion. "I know what it's like. I understand how difficult it can be to do something purely on principle. It wasn't easy fighting my stepfather for custody of Brian."

He seemed to relax now that the subject had veered slightly off of him.

Gwen stared at the horizon. "To this day, Robert has never admitted to having a problem. He beat Brian black and blue more times than anyone will probably ever know, but he refused to believe that his actions were wrong. To the very end, he tried to tell the judge that a man has a right to discipline his son in any way he chooses."

She sighed. "If he'd owned up to what he did, maybe my brother wouldn't have spent so many years thinking he deserved the treatment that was doled out to him.''

Anger rose up in her like an unexpected squall, lashing her with furious winds and bitter rains. She murmured, "I wish the state had prosecuted the bastard."

Nathan spoke for the first time. "You got Brian away from an awful situation. That's the important thing, isn't it?"

Feeling his eyes on her, she swung her gaze to his.

"Know this, Gwen," he said softly, "no one gets away with anything. There is an ancient Kolheek saying—if a man plants corn, he will eat in abundance. If he plants weeds, he will choke and starve when winter comes. Your stepfather has spent his life planting weeds."

For some reason, this idea calmed her. Soothed her anger. Many cultures believe in karma, she thought. Kismet. That one's destiny relies heavily on one's behavior. Making the right choices. Treating one's fellow man with fairness, with kindness, with love. And those who don't ultimately had to pay for their ill deeds.

The idea of a higher judgment appealed to Gwen. She liked to think that someone or something bigger, an omnipotent being, would take care of exacting vengeance. Requiring penance. Settling scores. This notion left her free to focus on her own behavior, her own choices.

After a moment she asked, "What makes a woman

choose, not one, but two life partners who are mean-spirited bullies?''

It only took Nathan a moment to figure out the direction of her query. ''You're speaking of your mother.''

She nodded silently in the twilight. ''After witnessing what Mom went through over the years, after learning from her about a woman's lot in life, I'd decided to avoid men. To avoid man-woman relationships—dating, marriage, all of that.'' She was aware of the mellifluous quality in her tone when she said, ''Until I met you.''

Revealing all these intimate details about her life—about herself—was clear evidence of how much she trusted him. Never before had she been so free with such personal and confidential information.

''Gwen...'' He squirmed uncomfortably as he straightened in the old wooden rocker.

Talking about the two of them wasn't at all what she'd planned to do. She'd honestly meant to honor Nathan's wish, even though she knew that her own feelings, desires and wishes were in direct contradiction to his. However, there was something deep inside that needed release. She didn't intend to be pushy. She only wanted to speak her mind. And something bone-deep, no, *heart-deep* was urging her to do just that.

''Nathan, I understand how you feel...about us,'' she told him. ''I really do. But I have to tell you, I think there are a few little holes in your logic.''

He set his half-empty beer mug on the wide porch

railing and scrubbed a hand over his jaw. It was obvious to Gwen that he didn't want to go into this. But she'd started it. She needed to finish it.

"You don't want to get involved in a relationship," she continued, "because you're afraid that, being a cop, you could die unexpectedly. Well—" she shrugged "—any one of us could die unexpectedly. I mean, I could step off a curb and get hit by a bus."

The muscle spanning his forehead tightened creating tiny creases in his sun-burnished skin. "Public buses don't run on the rez."

She rolled her eyes. "You know what I mean. Don't pretend you don't. I could cross the street at the wrong time and get killed by a car. A pickup truck. An SUV. Whatever. The point I'm trying to make is, none of us know when we're going to leave this world. None of us."

Nathan felt as if every tendon and muscle in his body was as tense as a coiled spring. Arguing about his motive for remaining single and unattached was the last thing he wanted to do.

Then he saw it. The unspoken question in her eyes. She was probing the possibility of a future for them.

Surprisingly his chest filled with pride and a joy that was unimaginable. A man would have to be dumb as dirt and made of stone not to feel uplifted by the notion that a woman like Gwen wanted him.

She was a beautiful woman. An intelligent woman. She fulfilled his every need. He loved her smile. He loved her laugh. He loved her quick wit. He loved the way she looked at him. He loved her lips. Her kiss. Her touch. Her...

His eyes went wide and he shook his head to rid his mind of the thoughts rolling and churning and teasing him with what he could so easily have—if he was to but reach out and seize them. She was right there. Well within his grasp.

"Look, Gwen," he said, disliking the harshness of his tone, yet unable to quell it, "I realize what you're saying. You're right. None of us can know when we'll go meet the Great One. But my fear is that my job as a police officer puts me into positions that..."

Images floated into his brain, images that were so distressing to him that the rest of his sentence simply disappeared into oblivion.

Sobbing women dressed in black. Innocent, grief-stricken children who would never know their fathers. Then he thought about the icy terror that had frozen his blood when he felt the cold steel of that knife make contact with his flesh.

The superficial wound he'd suffered in the line of duty could very well have been worse had he not moved swiftly enough. Had he not seen the glint of light against metal, he could be dead right now.

He would never make her understand his feelings. Never. His voice was tight as he said, "I think I should go."

Gwen evidently had other plans. "I have one more thing to ask, and then I'll leave this alone."

The resolve in her eyes told him he wouldn't get

away without hearing what she had to say, so he simply watched her lovely face and waited.

"What about Charity?"

Her chin had tipped up challengingly as the question rolled from her lips.

"You can't hold her at bay. You can't shield yourself from a relationship with her."

There was clear accusation in Gwen's words that conveyed this woman knew he had deep feelings for her and that he was refusing to surrender to the emotions he felt.

Well, that was true. It really was. But it didn't change his determination one iota.

"The fact that Charity is in my life—that she'd be left all alone if something were to happen to me—is a real worry, Gwen. A real worry." He paused, then forced himself to look her directly in the eye as he firmly added, "I choose not to add to the worry I already have."

I choose not to add to the worry I already have.

Those words haunted her for days. Gwen knew Nathan believed that having her in his life in any way other than merely as a casual friend—acknowledging what he felt for her—would be adding to his concern.

He was making a conscious effort not to do that.

She reached down and yanked up a weed, root and all, from the small flower bed by the front door. Hearing the familiar clink of the chain on Brian's bicycle, she looked up and saw him peddling down the narrow street toward her.

Since the sessions at Joseph's had started, Charity had taken to following Brian around like a puppy. Charity had arrived over an hour ago to ask Brian to teach her to dribble a basketball. They'd practiced for a while and then he'd taken her home.

"You didn't leave her at her house alone, did you?" she asked Brian when he hopped off the bike and shoved down the kickstand.

"Nathan was there," he said. "He asked me in for a glass of iced tea. That's why the trip took me so long."

There was apology in her brother's voice, an explanation for why he hadn't returned home immediately as he'd told her he would.

Gwen smiled, wanting to let him know that all was okay. She tossed the weed on top of the pile of the others she'd picked, marveling at the change in Brian. The time he'd spent with Nathan and with Joseph had made an amazing difference in her brother's attitude, in his whole way of thinking.

"It's awfully nice of you to spend so much time with Charity," she said softly. "You don't have to, you know."

Brian shrugged. "I don't mind. It's almost like having a kid sister." Then he grinned. "I sorta like how she looks up to me."

Had it really been just a couple of weeks ago that he'd spoken to her so hatefully? That he'd acted so rebelliously? The miraculous change in him reminded her of an ugly caterpillar metamorphosing into a beautiful butterfly. His transformation wasn't complete, but he was well on his way to becoming an amazing young man.

Remembering Nathan's concern about his daughter and Charity's lack of interest in anything feminine, Gwen said, "Maybe the next time she comes over we can get her to do something...different. Like...ah, baking cookies or sewing a pretty apron. I wouldn't mind showing her how."

Brian laughed. "I'm sure she'd rather run around playin' hide-'n'-seek than bake cookies. And I can't picture her ever wearing an apron, let alone making one."

Gwen grimaced and her brows raised heavenward. "Tell me about it!" She finally broke down and told her brother about Nathan's distress over Charity's partiality to tomboyish pastimes.

After listening to her, Brian was quiet, evidently pondering. Finally he said, "You know, Gwen, plenty of girls aren't interested in girl stuff. I mean, look at Sally Ride. She was the first woman to go into space. And there was that pilot, Amelia Earhart. She flew planes when women weren't pilots. I'm sure there's lots of women who have never baked a single cookie yet contribute to society in some way."

He combed his fingers through his wiry red hair. "Girls can do anything, Gwen," he continued. "Charity should be allowed to do the things she likes to do. Find her own way. Make her own dreams. If boys are encouraged to go after what they want, shouldn't girls be encouraged to do the same thing?"

Gwen sat back on her heels and just stared. She'd

spent all her college years learning that each child was an individual with gifts and talents all his or her own. However, it took her thirteen-year-old brother to remind her. Sometimes a person was too close to a problem to see things clearly.

Finally she shook her head in wonder and smiled. "How did you get so smart?" she asked.

She saw something glimmer in his eyes—pride, she quickly discerned—and it was a sight to behold. She and Brian shared a warm moment of silence before he trotted up the front steps toward the door, murmuring something about having homework that needed doing.

Nathan sat behind the steering wheel, waiting for his daughter to come out of Joseph's house. His grandfather's meetings with the children and teens of the reservation were more successful than Nathan had ever imagined they would be.

Incidences of petty vandalism on the rez had decreased. Store owners complained less of loitering teens. There were more kids participating in activities offered at the Community Center.

Now Nathan wasn't naive enough to think that all the youth problems could be solved by putting teens in touch with their past, but he did know that giving them a firm anchor into who they were and where they came from was a great beginning. Once kids discovered that their forefathers were honorable and brave and moral, it forced them to take a look at their own lives, ponder what kind of legacy they wanted to leave.

It seemed that Gwen's problem with her rebellious brother had actually helped everyone living at Smoke Valley. In attempting to tame Brian's unruly nature, Nathan had luckily latched on to a plan that seemed to be benefiting lots of the rez teens and the younger Kolheek children, as well.

Gwen. Her beautiful face swam before his closed eyelids. The sunlight had a way of catching her hair, transforming it to coppery flames. Her eyes were green as emeralds, and he'd even gotten close enough on a couple of occasions to know that they were flecked with a warm, golden hue.

He remembered the times he'd touched her silky skin, kissed her delectable mouth. His body flushed with heat and he felt the need to gulp in some of the cool night air.

Leaning his head back against the headrest, he opened his eyes wide and sighed heavily. He needed to banish these thoughts from his brain. Battling his hormones, his own selfish wants and desires, was the hardest thing he'd had to face since arriving on the reservation—since meeting one sexy first-grade teacher named Miss Gwen Fleming.

He thought about their last meeting. About how she'd reasoned against the choices he was making—the choices he was forcing on her. It had been obvious that she'd wanted to continue their relationship.

Oh, how he'd have loved to take her in his arms right there on the porch. How he'd have loved to...

But that would have been a mistake. Luckily he'd recognized it then just as he did now. In the end he'd told her flat out that having her in his life was a choice he wasn't willing to make.

He was certain she understood his motives. She might not agree with them, but she understood them. That was all that mattered. Well, that and his winning the battle over his own libido. Oh, how he wanted her! Even now he nearly groaned with the desire that had his blood pulsing thickly.

What he found most amazing was that he didn't have to be with her physically to suffer this overwhelming yearning. Thoughts alone were enough to trigger—

The tiny hairs on the back of his neck rose, and his skin came alive as a shivery chill raced down his arms, over his torso. Awareness. He was alert, body and mind, as he scanned the darkness surrounding the vehicle.

Then he saw her walking down the street toward his grandfather's home—toward *him.* She stopped at the gate, glancing at her wristwatch—a habit, he guessed, because there was no way she could see it in the darkness. Her gaze took in the front of the house, the lights in the windows, lingering on the front door. Evidently she hadn't seen Nathan parked nearby.

He should stay away. He should remain right where he...

The air was warm for September in New England, he noticed as he opened the door. It felt like heated satin against his face as he exited the vehicle and made his way down the short expanse of asphalt. There was something magical dancing all around him, fireworks exploding in the sky overhead that were invisible to everyone's eyes but his own, and the strange enchantment swirling in the night air had him feeling woozy. Reckless.

This out-of-control feeling filled him with fear—and an indescribable exhilaration.

She saw him before he'd closed the distance between them, and her initial reaction was a smile so bright he'd thought night had turned to day. His whole body filled with elation.

But then her gaze clouded, as if in an instant she remembered their awkward situation—that they both suffered an unbearable attraction to each other and he was unwilling to surrender himself to it. It was obvious she felt highly discomfited by such a state of affairs, and that saddened Nathan.

"Ah, Gwen—" the words slipped from his tongue in a tone swarming with silky sensuousness "—please don't look at me like that."

The ill-at-ease expression on her face changed, then, to ire.

"What do you want from me, Nathan?"

Her lustrous curls bobbed when she shook her head in seeming confusion. Or was it frustration?

"You know how I feel about you," she said. "I've made things perfectly clear. And you've made your plan perfectly plain, as well. It isn't right for you to expect me to…to…'' She lifted both hands, palm heavenward. "What is it you expect from me, anyway? To greet you as an old friend? To pretend that you didn't steal my heart right out of my chest? To act as if—"

When he reached out and smoothed the backs of his fingers down her jaw, it was as if he'd sliced her sentence in two with a razor-sharp hatchet, so quickly did she fall silent.

A hot current shot across his flesh, stimulating every nerve ending in his body. Making physical contact with her had been a dreadful mistake, he knew it. But he didn't give a damn.

Reckless. Rash. Wild.

Those were perfect words to describe what was rushing through him in this instant.

"Why do you have to be so beautiful?" He whispered the query, dragging the pad of his thumb lightly over her full bottom lip. He felt her quiver beneath his touch. "You intrigue me like no woman ever has. Even when you're angry with me, I want you."

Her green gaze searched his face. It was obvious that she might have been anticipating many different responses to her angry questions, but *this* hadn't been one of them.

Myriad emotions crossed her delicate features. Bewilderment. Uncertainty. Hope.

"D-does this mean you've changed your mind?"

Her voice was husky, and so sexy that Nathan felt his body physically respond in ways he didn't dare admit. The expectation in her question was both eager and guarded, and it was nearly his undoing. All he wished for was the taste of her lips, the feel of her beneath his hands.

But this was wrong. The devil himself had taken possession of Nathan's thoughts and desires. Either that or the love he felt for Gwen was deeper and stronger than he was.

Nathan was committed to his conviction to remain single. Or...he *thought* he was.

Oh, help me, he silently prayed to the Great Spirit.

However, it seemed as if his prayer simply floated away, unheard, unanswered, on the mountain breeze.

"If ever there was a woman who might change a man's mind," he said, weaving his fingers into her thick tresses, "that woman would be you."

His mind was in total chaos when he covered her mouth with his. She tasted of heat and honey, and Nathan wanted nothing more than to get lost in this most sumptuous moment. He felt enveloped by the night. Swathed in the powerful need that thumped through him like the rhythm of some ancient drum, matching the beat of his heart.

Gwen. Gwen. In that instant, she filled him. Mind. Body. Soul.

She smelled of sunshine and wildflowers. Her skin was velvet. Her hair, feather-soft. Her lips were moist. Hot. Yielding.

He wanted to spirit her away from this too-public street where any passerby could see them. He wanted to go someplace quiet. Private. He wanted to satiate the craving that had seemed to well up out of nowhere and drive him half crazy.

Slowly, laboriously, as if through a viscous haze, something dawned on him. Gwen wasn't touching him. Her arms weren't around him. Her hands weren't kneading or sliding or urging, as his were. What they were doing was hanging limp at her sides.

Oh, she'd enjoyed their kiss just as much as he. Her breath had quickened, and he'd even heard her moan against his mouth at one point. However, it was clear that she was doing all she could to control herself. She was using great restraint.

He looked down into her lovely face, blinking his way out of the rapturous fog that had ensnared him as he searched her gem-green eyes.

Gwen attempted to avoid his gaze, but he wouldn't let her. He curled his index finger, nestled it beneath her chin and tipped it up so that she was forced to look at him. Finally the discomfort she felt evidently became more than she could tolerate and she stepped away from him.

There was quiet resolve in her tone when she said, "You say I'm the kind of woman who *might* change a man's mind—"

Even though her tone sounded grating and dry, the emphasis wasn't lost on him.

"—but," she continued, "you weren't clear about whether or not you have changed your mind."

Silence was Nathan's only recourse.

"I didn't think so," she whispered. Shadowy gloom seemed to fall around them like a wet blanket. Then a tiny frown bit into her brow. Her voice was stronger now as she asked, "How fair are you being to me, Nathan?"

Emotions sprang up, walloping him like a hammer between the eyes. Guilt. Remorse. Distress.

Gwen was right. How fair was he being to her?

As determined as he'd been only a moment before to connect with her gaze, now he couldn't keep his eyes from sliding, reproachfully, to the ground.

"I'm sorry, Gwen," he murmured. Reaching up, he scrubbed agitated fingers across the back of his neck. "There's no excuse for my behavior. No excuse."

"You're right," she agreed. "There isn't."

He forced himself to look at her. The agony he felt over his lack of self-restraint escalated.

"All I can tell you," he continued, desperation heavy in his voice, "is that you've gotten under my skin. You're in my thoughts. In my dreams. I can't escape you, no matter how hard I try." Unable to quell his tongue, he said, "You're in my blood, Gwen."

She was quiet for several seconds. Challenge set her jaw. "Yet you're still determined not to commit yourself to a relationship."

Confusion reigned in his chaotic thoughts. He wanted to say yes. He wanted to say no. Hell, he didn't know how to respond.

Shouts and squeals had both their heads turning to see Joseph's front door open, teens and younger children pouring out onto the lawn.

Softly Gwen said to Nathan, "I can live with being

just your friend. But I won't allow you to toy with my feelings."

That mallet of guilt slammed into him again, this time straight to the gut.

"I—"

"Dad!"

Charity raced to her father and jumped into his arms, making it impossible for Nathan to assure Gwen that playing games with her emotions was the last thing he'd meant to do...that the kiss they had just shared was as much a surprise to him as it was to her...that he'd been spellbound by—

"Hey, Gwen," Brian called out to his sister, "can Richard come have ice cream with us?"

The smile she offered her brother was bright, but Nathan could see the shadows still clouding her lovely eyes. Shame filled him to know that he'd put them there.

"Sure," she told Brian. "Your friend is more than welcome to come with us."

The boys jogged across the grass to join them.

Gwen said, "We should probably go so we can get to the shop before it closes." She glanced at Charity, evidently working to keep her tone cheerful. "I'll see *you* in school tomorrow, young lady."

Charity grinned. "I'll see you, too." She giggled. Then the child turned to her daddy. "Let's go home, Dad. You promised to read to me tonight, remember?"

"Of course, I remember. How could I forget a thing like that?"

Like Gwen had succeeded in doing, Nathan put on a mask of lightheartedness, even though his heart was anything but light. Taking Charity's hand, he headed toward the car, but not before turning to watch Gwen walk away from him without a backward glance.

Chapter Nine

The narrow streets of Smoke Valley Reservation were lined with booths, tables, even tents, featuring all manner of Native American arts and crafts. Moccasins, belts, vests, dresses, some plain, some adorned with shells or colorful beads, were on display. Authentic Kolheek pottery of all shapes and sizes was for sale, decorated with geometric shapes in mellow earth tones. Oil and acrylic paintings of day-to-day Indian life, now and in the past, hung beside muted watercolors. The exquisite quilts Gwen saw must have taken hours and hours to create. One stall offered hand carved wooden figures with facial features so realistic she actually expected the tiny statues to start talking as she passed by.

The steady stream of cars along the streets, their drivers searching for places to park, and the crowds milling about the tables and tents of the various artisans was a clear sign that people from all over New England were visiting the Fall Craft Festival.

"What *is* that delicious smell?"

Gwen laughed as her brother's plaintive question was followed up with an audible rumble from his evidently empty stomach. She reached into her purse and rummaged around for a few bills. "Go find out what it is," she told him, giving him the money. "And bring me back something to eat when you come. I won't go far."

He grinned his thanks. "Don't worry, I'll find you." Then he disappeared into the crowd of people on his search for their lunch.

Turning to admire the hand-tooled leather purses, Gwen bumped into Mattie Russell.

"Gwen! How are you?"

Mattie owned a bed-and-breakfast she called Freedom Trail. Gwen's heart warmed with gratitude, and she hugged her friend tightly.

"I haven't seen you since school started, have I?" Gwen asked. "I should have stopped by the inn for a visit. What kind of a friend am I? And after all you've done for me. I should be ashamed."

"Oh, now—" Mattie shushed her with a wave of her hand "—you've been busy with a new job and a new home. Not to mention Brian. How are things going for you two?"

"Wonderfully!" Gwen had Mattie to thank for the new life she and Brian were enjoying. Mattie was in her midtwenties, Gwen guessed. She was a thin, willowy beauty, but without the young woman's quiet yet formidable inner strength, Gwen didn't think she'd have survived those awful weeks of fighting her stepfather for legal custody of her brother.

The two women stood on the sidewalk sharing some of what had been going on in their lives, and, Gwen was careful not to mention the dilemma she'd experienced with Nathan. The man was stubborn as a pack mule, yet there wasn't a thing she could do about it. The passionate kiss he'd planted on her lips just a few nights ago had made her knees go weak. That same kiss had also revealed, unequivocally, his true feelings for her. But Gwen refused to fight a losing battle. And sadly she'd been forced to conclude, once again, that Nathan's will had truly won the war he was having with his emotions. He'd beat down his feelings but good.

"Mattie, look what I found."

The stranger who approached the two of them was a young woman of about the same age as Mattie, Gwen surmised. Her honey-brown hair glistened in the fall sunshine, and although her delicate features were upturned in a smile, there was an unmistakable sadness about her. Gwen's gaze lowered to the small swell of the young woman's belly, and her curiosity was sparked regarding what might cause such melancholy at what should be a time of great joy and fulfillment for any woman.

Mattie examined the colorfully beaded bracelet the woman held up for inspection.

"It's beautiful," Mattie told her. "I'm glad you're allowing yourself to have some fun. You deserve it."

Mattie looked at Gwen. "Gwen, I'd like you to meet Lori Young. She's a nurse." Mattie's voice lowered conspiratorially as she said, "Lori's staying with me at the moment."

Lori's head automatically swiveled, almost as if she was searching the crowd for an intruder. Gwen got the distinct impression that Lori felt danger was close at hand. Something akin to fear shadowed the woman's chestnut-hued eyes and Gwen's heart went out to her.

"It's okay," Mattie said, calming Lori with a pat on her forearm. "Gwen stayed with me, too, for a bit."

Lori's gaze lit on Gwen's face, and Gwen smiled reassuringly. Nothing brought people together like trouble shared.

"You can trust Mattie," Gwen told Lori. "She'll help you just as she helped me. I've got a lovely home now. And a great job."

Mattie grinned. "That's what I'm working on for Lori right now. A job. I heard that Dr. Grey Thunder needs a nurse." Her smile widened mischievously. "And have I got a nurse for him!"

Gwen couldn't help but join in with Mattie's laughter, but she didn't fail to notice that poor Lori looked less than hopeful about whatever situation she found herself in.

Just then Charity raced up to Gwen.

"Hi, Ms. Fleming," the child greeted, excitement lacing her tone. "I didn't know you were coming to the festival."

"I wouldn't have missed it, sweetie," Gwen said. "I enjoy shopping, just like every woman does."

Charity's nose wrinkled. "I hate shopping. But later my granddaddy's going to tell some stories. There's going to be dancing and everything. At the Community Center. That'll be really neat, don'tcha think? Will you be there?"

"Yes," Gwen agree said. "I wouldn't miss it."

An evening steeped in Native American culture sounded right up her alley. Brian had been as excited telling her about the events planned for this evening as Charity seemed to be right now, and that made Gwen smile.

Gwen took the opportunity to introduce the child to Mattie and Lori, and the three exchanged greetings.

"Where's Brian?" the little girl asked Gwen.

"He's supposed to be buying me some lunch." She scanned the ever-growing mob for her brother. Then realizing that Charity wasn't with an adult, she asked, "Where's your father? You shouldn't be on your own. There are too many strangers on the rez today for you to be safe."

"I'm staying with Great-granddaddy today," she told Gwen. Her little chest seemed to puff out as she added, "My dad is working. It's a special day, so all the policemen, er, ah…policewomen…um…all the police people…"

Charity paused in her explanation, clearly flummoxed by what she wanted to say and the inadequate words that were coming to her mind.

"You mean officers?" Gwen suggested.

The girl's gaze lit up at the non-gender-specific description. "Yes!" she pronounced. "All the officers have to work today. And my dad is the boss of every single one of them."

The three woman shared a smile at the child's pride in her father. Charity's face beamed even brighter when the very man she'd just been speaking of approached the group.

"What are you doing, young lady?" Nathan chided his daughter. "You're supposed to be with your great-grandfather. He's standing over by the ice-cream booth and he's worried about where you ran off to."

Something extraordinary happened to Gwen just seeing Nathan in his police uniform. Her insides went all atwitter and her skin seemed to tingle with awareness. Funny, the uniform he wore used to frighten her, she remembered. Now that she knew the man, his attire—or rather, the body beneath the attire—stirred her desire.

The expression on Charity's face was filled to the brim with innocence. "I was just saying hello to Ms. Fleming."

"Well, you need to tell someone where you're going *before* you go off, do you understand?"

Charity kicked at the sidewalk with the toe of her sneaker. "Okay, I will. I promise." Her tone was apologetic. "I'll go let Great-granddaddy know I'm okay."

"Hold on," Nathan said, snagging Charity's hand before she could dart away from him. "This crowd is too big. I want you to wait for me. I'll take you to Joseph."

The child sulked in silence and Nathan turned his attention to Gwen, Mattie and Lori.

"Hi, Gwen," he said.

Not missing the contrite quality in Nathan's voice, Gwen hated that their relationship had evolved into this awkward mess.

"Mattie," he said, nodding a pleasant greeting. Then he waited to be introduced to Lori.

Mattie didn't disappoint him. "Nathan, I'd like you to meet Lori. She's going to be your brother's saving grace. She's a nurse, and I heard that a nurse is just what Dr. Grey is looking for."

Nathan grinned, evidently realizing that Mattie was on a mission. "Nice to meet you, Lori." Then he turned to Mattie. "You can find Grey at the medical tent. He volunteered his services today."

"Well, thank you for the information," Mattie said. She took Lori's arm, but just as Gwen thought the two woman were going to take their leave, Mattie turned back to Nathan. "One more thing," she said, her brow knitting with sudden concern, "I've seen a man on the far side of Smoke Lake. Near my house, actually. I suspect he's staying at the old hunting lodge. He's not bothering me. He's just…there. Do you know who he might be?"

Nathan was quiet for a moment. Then he leveled his dark eyes on Mattie's face. "I'm sure everything's okay. You don't have anything to worry about. But

I'll look into it, Mattie. I'll go out there right away and check it out.''

But Nathan's careful choice of words was an unmistakable indication to Gwen that he knew more than he was willing to admit.

"Thanks, Nathan," Mattie said. "I do appreciate it. A woman living alone can't be too careful, you know?" She tapped Lori on the shoulder. "Let's go find the good doctor," she told the young woman. "We're going to get you a job. Bye, Gwen. See you around, Nathan."

They waved as they stepped off the curb to cross the street.

Curiosity got the best of Gwen. "You know who it is, don't you? The man Mattie was asking about?"

For a moment, she thought Nathan might not tell her what she already knew was the truth. But then his lips pursed and he sighed.

"It's my cousin, Conner," Nathan said. "He's been staying at the cabin. He's, ah…laying low."

He didn't want her asking any questions, Gwen realized. So she didn't. But her interest was truly piqued now. Did he mean that his cousin was hiding from the law? Was the man in some kind of trouble? But how could Nathan—the sheriff of Smoke Valley— allow such a situation to develop or continue? Nathan's sense of right and wrong was stronger than that of anyone Gwen had ever met, so that left her wondering if his cousin could have dropped out of sight for some other reason.

Questions rolled through her head, but she could tell she'd get no answers from Nathan.

"Can we go find Great-granddaddy now?" Charity's plaintive question was followed by a sharp tug on her father's pant leg.

"Sure, honey. Let's go." Nathan looked at Gwen. "Would you like to walk along with us?"

"I'd love to see Joseph," she said, "but I promised Brian I'd wait here for him."

"But he was with my grandfather when I left him just a minute ago."

"Oh." Gwen smiled down at Charity. "Then I guess I should just come along with you, then."

"All right," Charity said, "let's go find my buddy Brian!" She danced in place. "It's awful hard for me to keep still for very long."

Nathan chuckled. "Yes, I know that, little one. I sure do know that."

They had only walked a few steps when Charity grumbled, "I feel like I'm swimmin' in a sea of knees and feet."

"Well, here," Nathan said, "maybe this will help." He picked up his daughter and plunked her down on his shoulders.

The child squealed with glee. "I can see everything from up here, Dad."

"Careful, now," he warned her. "Those aren't doorknobs on the sides of my head. They're my ears. And I'd like to keep them right where they are, if you don't mind."

"Oh, Dad—" Charity giggled "—you're funny."

After only a moment the child blurted, "Dad, how come I don't look like you do?"

Gwen felt rather than saw Nathan tense beside her, and both of them slowed their steps.

"What do you mean, honey?" he asked Charity.

"Well, I don't look like the Kolheeks here on the rez," she said without hesitation. "I don't look like Great-granddaddy. Or Uncle Grey. You and Uncle Grey have straight black hair. So does most everyone else here. My hair's all curly. Your skin is dark. Mine's white...just like Ms. Fleming's is."

Although Gwen remained silent, she couldn't stop her gaze from traveling to Nathan's face as she wondered how he would respond to his daughter's inquiry.

He was quiet for a bit, and finally he softly said, "Charity, you're the image of your mother. You have her hair. Her eyes. You even have her laugh." Reaching up, he patted her reassuringly on the knee. "You and I don't need to have the same color skin or the same hair texture for me to be your dad. All we need is love for each other."

A smile tugged at the corners of Gwen's mouth. He couldn't have given Charity a better answer, she thought.

"Well," the child pressed, "Brian and Ms. Fleming are related and they have the same kind of hair. Ain't it strange that I don't have your nose, or your ears, or your...well, or your anything."

"*Isn't* it strange," Nathan corrected her.

"That's just what I said. It's *very* strange, don'tcha think?"

Gwen pressed her fingers to her mouth to keep her from laughing. But when she looked at Nathan, she saw that he wasn't finding this conversation the least bit amusing.

A sudden realization hit her, and she instantly sobered. Lord above, why hadn't she seen the truth before? It had been plain as the light of day all along.

Nathan lifted Charity from her perch and set her down on the sidewalk. Then he squatted down so that he was on eye level with her.

"Honey, I love you," he said. "And you love me. For right now I think that's enough to hold us together." The tap he gave the tip of her little nose was light and loving. "Forever and ever."

Charity's mouth curled up in a grin. "Okay, Dad. Forever and ever."

Father and daughter shared a smile—his, doting, hers, adoring. Then Nathan stood, planted his hands on Charity's shoulders and turned her around to face away from him.

"Now, there's your great-grandfather," he told the child. "Go over there and apologize for running off without telling him."

"Yes, sir!" Charity scampered off.

Gwen knew she was holding her breath. Finally she could stand it no longer.

"You're not her biological father," she breathed.

He hesitated only a moment before softly admitting, "No, I'm not."

She watched his jaw muscle work and guessed that the thoughts running through his head were bothersome.

"I think it's too soon to tell her," Nathan continued. "I want our relationship to be good and strong first."

That was easy enough to understand. Gwen asked, "Where is her father? How come he didn't come forward to take Charity?"

"I don't know." He shrugged. "I don't know who the man is. Or where he is. I seriously doubt Ellen even knew who fathered Charity."

"That's so sad." Gwen shook her head. "But the woman must have had parents. Siblings. *Someone.*"

"The fact that she called *me,*" he said, "a man she hadn't seen in years, was a pretty clear indication that she had no one else to turn to. I went through her apartment, Gwen. Searched her belongings. I found not one scrap of information about her family or who might have fathered Charity."

Gwen's steps slowed and then stopped altogether. "But you changed your whole life. Quit your job. Moved to Vermont. And all for a child who doesn't even belong to you."

He was pensive. Finally he explained, "Ellen was dying. I didn't see any other choice but to make her last days a little easier by taking away her worry about Charity."

There had to be more to this. "But…" Feeling that further probing might be seen as intrusive, Gwen let the rest of her thought fade away.

Nathan sighed. "Gwen, as a Kolheek I've been taught the importance of paying back debts. Unselfishly. And without thought of personal impact. You see, I lost my parents when I was young. If my grandfather hadn't stepped up and taken responsibility for me, I'd have been out in the cold. Living on the streets. Just as Charity would have been had I not done the right thing."

Doing the right thing. Making the right choices. Planting corn, instead of weeds. Those were very important aspects of who and what Nathan Thunder was.

The fact that he had changed his whole life for a little girl he hadn't even known existed before he'd received that fateful call on behalf of his fatally ill ex-girlfriend...

Gwen thought her heart would simply shatter into a million shards, so full was it with the love she felt for this man. He was extraordinary. A truly remarkable individual.

And she wished with all her might that she could tell him so. But...he'd made that quite impossible.

That same evening, Nathan was patrolling the streets, relieved to see that the crowd had thinned. He was tired. He and his whole crew of officers had had a long and demanding day.

There had been several incidences of petty theft, and Nathan had actually escorted several teens off reservation land for fighting. A sobbing three-year-old boy had become separated from his parents. And an elderly woman had slipped, bruising her elbow badly enough that Nathan had to call an ambulance to come from the neighboring town of Mountview to take her to hospital for X rays.

All he could think about was getting this day over with so he could go home and step into a nice, hot shower.

Now, now, a small voice chided from somewhere in the back of his brain, *that's not* all *you can think about.*

A rueful grin tugged at one corner of his mouth and he shook his head in helpless agreement.

Gwen.

She'd been planted firmly in his thoughts all day long. He'd seen her, off and on, during the festivities. And ever since she'd discovered he wasn't Charity's biological father, something had…changed. She'd been treating him differently.

Gwen had been cool toward him, and she had good reason for such an attitude. He'd treated her terribly, withholding his emotions one moment and then surrendering to his urge to kiss her the next. It was a wonder she hadn't slapped him silly that night. Yet she hadn't. What she had done was told him off. Soundly. And then she'd retreated into a shell meant to protect herself. A shell he had no business trying to crack.

However, since finding out earlier today that Charity wasn't his blood daughter, Gwen had blessed him with an endearing smile each and every time they passed on the streets. It was almost as if she'd forgiven him all his past sins.

He hadn't revealed the information regarding his relationship to Charity to get into Gwen's good graces. Heck, the woman had already guessed his secret. He'd only confirmed it.

He spied Gwen then, just down the block. She waved, her mouth curving warmly, and Nathan felt his blood heat.

Women sure were amazing creatures. And Gwen was no exception. Apparently his stepping up to the plate and taking full responsibility for Charity—an act in which he felt he had no real choice—had apparently caused Gwen to make allowances for all his shortcomings.

He watched as she swung her head to one side, tossing her thatch of glorious copper curls over her shoulder. The thought struck him for what seemed the billionth time—if ever there was a woman who could change a man's mind...

His heart seemed to swell in his chest as tender and achy emotion inflated inside him. How on earth would he ever hold on to his convictions?

The question barely had time to shift through his mind before his whole world tipped off-kilter. The horrifying scene before him seemed to unfold in slow motion.

A rough-looking man approached an unsuspecting Gwen from the alley between the buildings. He jerked her purse from her shoulder and then shoved her. Violently. Gwen didn't even have time to cry out before she fell to the ground, her packages tumbling and rolling helter-skelter all around her.

Nathan's blood seemed to freeze in his veins, and it was a moment before he got his feet to obey the commands of his brain. He tore down the street with one thought and one thought alone ricocheting in his skull.

Protect Gwen.

Pain shot through Gwen's body. Her right shoulder ached terribly and her knee burned like fire. She heard shouting, but the voices sounded muffled, dreamlike and far off. There was movement around her, but it was disjointed and out of focus. Everything had happened so quickly. One moment she'd been walking down the street, the next she was lying flat on her face with the day's purchases scattered about.

She rolled onto her side and attempted to sit up. Her wrist throbbed when she put weight on her hand, and she sucked in a lungful of air. Something at the periphery of her vision had her darting a glance just in time to see a man racing away from her. Her eyes widened in wonder. Was that her brand-new leather purse clutched under his arm like a football?

The man disappeared from sight, darting around the corner of the market, as the realization struck her—she'd been robbed!

Stunned, she simply sat on the pavement, blinking back the tears that seemed determined to leak from her eyes, taking some deep, calming breaths so she could get back in sync with the here and now. She saw Nathan sprinting toward her and talking into his handheld radio. He was summoning help, she suspected. That was good because she could use a little help about now.

"Gwen!" Nathan crouched next to her. "You okay?"

Still too stupefied to answer right away, she just stared at him. Took in his high cheekbones, his smooth, dusky skin, his dark, luscious eyes. She couldn't help but think that he must be the most handsome man on the face of the earth. Strange that such a thought would ramble through the incoherence of her mind. Finally she murmured, "I'm alive."

He gripped her upper arms, and pain rolled over her in a wave. She must have winced because let her go.

"My shoulder," she said.

"I'll get you to the medical tent. My brother's there. He'll take a look at you, see if anything's broken."

The tenderness in Nathan's voice melted her heart. The tears she'd been fighting gushed and spilled down her cheeks unchecked.

"Oh, honey," he said, smoothing the pads of his fingers along her jaw, "please don't cry. It's all over."

His touch brought her whole body alive.

His gaze swept the length of her and he inhaled sharply. "You're bleeding."

She realized then that her jeans were torn at the knee and a cherry-red stain on the fabric was slowly spreading.

Nathan's dark gaze turned flinty. "The bastard will pay for this, don't you worry."

Two officers struggled toward them, the hand-cuffed purse snatcher jerking and pulling at the hold they had on his arms.

"Gwen! What happened?" Brian pushed his way to the front of the small group of people gathered on the street, Charity close on his heels.

"I'm okay, Brian," Gwen assured her brother. "I'll have a bruise or two, I'm sure, but everything's all right."

Nathan helped her to her feet, but spun away from her when he heard one of his officers shout in alarm. A scream froze in Gwen's throat when she saw the perpetrator kick one of the officers in the leg, causing the policeman to crumble to the ground, agony etched on his features. In a rage now, the purse snatcher slammed his body into the other officer, sending them both tumbling to the pavement. The handcuffs didn't prove much of a deterrent, so quickly was the man on his feet and racing away.

Moving with lightning speed, Nathan sprinted forward and tackled the man who had robbed her and caused her physical injury. The prisoner refused to relent, rolling to his feet and fighting Nathan with head and shoulder butts. He twisted out of Nathan's grasp, growling like some kind of crazed animal, spitting out vulgarities that would embarrass even the most hardened of people.

Gwen's mouth dropped open in horror when Nathan grabbed the thief and slammed him facedown to the ground, planting a knee between the man's shoulder blades and asserting enough pressure to elicit a cry of anguished surrender.

Seeing such violent and hostile behavior in Nathan shook Gwen to the core. Fear liquefied her knee joints, and she was acutely aware that her brother, with his background of abuse, was most assuredly feeling just as affected by the scene as she. And Charity! The poor child had probably never witnessed her father act this way, Gwen was certain.

She had to do something. She had to get Brian and Charity away from this disturbing situation. Away from this violence.

"I need you to help me get to the medical tent," she told the kids. But they remained motionless, mesmerized by the drama unfolding before them. Gwen raised her voice as she called them by name.

"Let's go," she said, waving them toward her with her good hand and doing her darnedest to ignore the scuffling and cursing going on just a few yards away. "Now!"

With her brother and Charity in tow, she limped away as quickly as she could.

Chapter Ten

The evening had finally grown quiet by the time Nathan could make his way to Gwen's house. He stood in the darkness, looking at the small bungalow, noting that the front windows were dark.

She was probably in bed. After her ordeal, he couldn't blame her for turning in early.

He should probably go away and come back tomorrow. But that was impossible. There were things that needed to be said. Emotions that needed to be exposed. Changes of heart that needed to be revealed.

When he'd witnessed that punk of a thief rip off Gwen's purse and viciously throw her to the ground, there had been one concept alone that his mind had been able to wrap around: *protect her.*

Like a flash of blinding light, he'd been struck with a marvelous realization. The love he felt for Gwen transcended all else. He loved her with all his heart. With all his soul. With every fiber of his being.

In the face of such magnitude of emotion, his conviction to remain unattached evaporated. And besides that, he realized just how stupid he'd been.

Gwen had been right all along. No one can predict when death will come. No one can hide from it. No one can sidestep it. But avoiding living life to the fullest because of a fear of death was wrong. Terribly wrong.

He knew the truth now. He knew that if he didn't spend the rest of his life with Gwen, the Great One might as well take him now, because he sure didn't want to live without her.

The soles of his shoes scuffed the stoop, and he raised his hand and knocked on the door. He regretted having to wake her, but he thought that, after hearing all he had to say, she wouldn't mind too much.

A soft smile still played on his mouth as she opened the door to him.

"Nathan."

Her delicate features were soft, the moonlight turning her hair silky, nearly iridescent. All he wanted to do was reach out and touch her. But he didn't. There was too much he wanted to tell her first, and if he surrendered to the urge to get physical, he just might end up botching the job.

"I came to make sure you're okay," he told her. Then he gave a nervous chuckle. "That's not the only reason I came. May I come in?"

She backed up a step or two so he could enter.

"I'm glad you came. I...I have something I need to tell you."

Her voice was soft, but the intensity he heard in the words had his gaze flying to her face.

Trouble seemed to knit her brow and his insides tightened instinctively.

Gwen closed the door and moved to the living room. "Sit down," she offered as she lowered herself into an armchair. "I've been tossing and turning, trying to sleep, but it's just no use."

"You're in pain?" he asked as he took a seat on the couch. "I'm so sorry."

She waved her hand in a small arc. "I took one of the painkillers your brother gave me. I'm not that hurt, actually. A bruised shoulder, sprained wrist. A scraped knee." She shook her head. "No, it's not my injuries that have kept me awake."

"You're upset," he guessed. "About what happened today."

"Well...yes. That would describe what I'm feeling."

Her green eyes held an emotion so intense that Nathan was held rapt by it.

"I've decided," she continued, "that you were right all along." She paused long enough to moisten her lips. "I think it really is for the best that our relationship isn't allowed to grow into something...more intimate."

Stunned wasn't a strong enough word to express how Nathan was feeling.

"Today, I felt..." The host of emotions rising to

the surface was evidently more than she could bear, and she paused long enough to take a deep breath. Then she unwittingly moistened her lips and began again.

"Today, I felt so afraid," she told him. Huskily she added, "Of you."

That truly shocked all thought from his head, and all he could do was sit there, helplessly mute.

"You said you'd make that man pay for hurting me." Her voice was small as she added, "And that's exactly what you did." She blinked, pursed her lips, guilt clear and unmistakable in her face. "You literally smashed that poor man to the pavement." Her eyes glistened with tears. "He was handcuffed, Nathan. You hurt him because of me."

Nathan wanted to defend himself. To justify his actions. But he couldn't get his tongue to work properly.

"You need to know something," Gwen continued. She laced her fingers together tightly. "My stepfather didn't just start beating up on Brian out of the blue one day. Robert's abusive behavior was first launched on my mom years before Brian was even born. I witnessed it, Nathan. I watched as his degrading comments turned to open-handed smacks and those smacks turned to closed-fisted punches. I saw the black eyes, the broken noses. I saw him beat my mother to a pulp. Body and soul."

Her indrawn breath was shaky. "The police came to our house more times than I could count."

She stopped long enough to swallow, evidently shaken by some thought.

"Your uniform. I was afraid of you when you showed up in my classroom wearing it." Gwen shook her head. "I know it makes no sense. The police always arrived with the idea of helping me and my mother, not harming us. But you see, seeing you in that uniform just brought back memories. Vivid memories of the things I'd endured growing up. Things I was helpless to stop."

Gwen sighed, squared her shoulders. "I didn't mean to get offtrack here. The point to all this is…I fear aggressive men, Nathan. I always have. And I always will."

Accusation tainted her green gaze as she leveled it, unwaveringly, on him.

"Wait a minute," he said. His head shook from side to side as he tried to grasp the equation she was setting up. "Wait just a minute. Are you saying…" The thought petered out as he mentally calculated. When he finally got the sum of her thoughts, anger flared. "I can't believe you're putting me in the same category as Brian's father!"

He expected her to look guilt-ridden, but her expression remained determined. Then his ire fizzled as mortification set in. To think she might have that opinion of him!

"Gwen," he began, carefully, "I'll admit I'm aggressive, even forceful sometimes. My job often calls for it." A small breath puffed from his chest. "But there's a distinct difference between my behavior and that of your stepfather.''

She looked unconvinced.

''I only use force to serve the public I'm bound to protect.'' Sudden agitation had him sliding his hands along his thighs, digging and kneading the muscles with his fingertips. ''That man robbed you today,'' he continued. ''He shoved you aside like a sack of garbage. Then he fled with no regard for your welfare.''

He paused long enough to let what he'd said sink in. ''But his treatment of you wasn't the only reason I took him down the way I did. He broke the law, Gwen. Plain and simple. And when my men caught him, he resisted arrest. He harmed my officers. Men who are under my supervision. Men I'm responsible for. I *had* to subdue him. He could have harmed some innocent bystander. He could have harmed me!''

He heard his tone escalating and knew the cause of it wasn't just anger. He was insulted. He slowed down long enough to garner control of his emotions.

Quieter now, he said, ''I won't let you lump me into the same category as the scumbag who brutalized your mother and your brother. There's no way I'm anything like him. When I show aggression, it's for a reason. A noble reason. Your stepfather abused those who were powerless against him, in some twisted attempt to make himself look bigger than he was.'' Nathan shook his head. ''He's a sorry excuse for a man.''

''He's right, Gwen.''

Both Nathan and Gwen swiveled their heads to see that Brian had entered the living room.

"Brian." Gwen stood up. "I'm sorry we woke you, but I really would appreciate it if you'd go back into your room so Nathan and I can—"

"You can't shut me out of this, Gwen," Brian said, raising his chin. "You're being unfair to Nathan. And it's wrong."

A frown furrowed Gwen's brow, and Nathan got the distinct impression that she was at a loss for words. Pressing her lips together tightly, she sat back down in one quick, jerky motion. Brian came over and sat next to Nathan on the couch.

The boy rested his elbows on his knees, a posture that seemed too mature for his age. "Dad treated Mom bad. Real bad." His voice came out in a rusty whisper. "And when she wasn't around to take it anymore, he turned all his meanness on me."

Nathan saw Gwen flinch and he suspected she was feeling remorseful about having stayed away from home...away from the problems there for so long, leaving her brother to face the brunt of it alone. Of course, she hadn't realized what was taking place behind those closed doors. She'd explained that. But Nathan could see she still felt guilty about what her brother had been forced to endure.

"Like Nathan said," Brian continued, "what Dad did to Mom and me, how he acted...he doesn't deserve to be called a man. He doesn't deserve my love or my respect."

Gwen scooted to the edge of the chair. "Brian,

honey, this is the first time you've…'' She paused, emotion visibly overcoming her. She swallowed and tried again. "All these weeks I've tried to get you to talk about…*him*…about how he treated you."

"I don't want to talk about it." The teen's throat convulsed and silent tears slipped down his face. "It was horrible. The man who was supposed to take care of me beat the crap outta me. What good does it do to talk about it?"

Nathan felt compelled to respond. "It is good to talk, Brian. Not only would you be letting out all your anger and resentment about the past, but you'd quickly discover that what happened to you wasn't your fault. You weren't to blame. You're a human being, worthy of respect, deserving of safety and love and kindness and caring. Just like everyone else."

Brian raised his head, his spine straightening with dignity. "You made me understand that. The weekend we were camping together. And Joseph's been telling me the same thing through his stories." He glanced from Nathan to Gwen. "You two might think I'm just a kid, but I've been storing away everything you've been teaching me."

The three of them continued to talk. About the past. About the present. And even a little about the future. Finally Brian apologized to his sister for lashing out at her all those weeks ago. He said he was glad that she'd brought him to Smoke Valley. That he was grateful to be where he could feel safe and loved. That he was grateful she'd fought for and won custody of him.

At last Brian got up and hugged Gwen. "I know it wasn't easy. I love you for all you've done."

Long minutes after Brian had bid them good-night and gone back his bedroom, Gwen's gaze remained trained on the hallway down which he'd disappeared.

"I can't believe it," she finally said. She turned to Nathan. "He's really going to be okay."

Nathan nodded. "He's healing."

She sighed. "I owe you an apology."

Her beautiful face screwed up with an expression that could only be described as something between contrition and embarrassment.

"A huge apology," she said.

"You don't owe me anything, Gwen." He realized that his anger had blown itself out completely. "I can understand why you'd be frightened of what you saw today. I really can."

There was a moment of awkwardness, but then she smiled at him and the awkwardness seemed to break up, scatter and dissolve. This was it, he realized. His chance to speak his heart. His opportunity to reveal what he'd come to tell her.

"I came tonight," he began, "so that I could talk to you. Tell you that..."

In that instant, his stomach muscles tensed. Shoving his anxiety aside, he plowed ahead. "I came to tell you that I...I think you've been right all along. I've had...well, I've had that change of heart you've been looking for."

She was silent. He had no clue what she was thinking. The disquiet that had been slowly churning in his gut now started to bubble and spit like thick goo simmering in a cauldron.

He rushed on, needing to get this speech over with. "I thought about some of the logic you brought up. You were right when you said that no one knows when they're going to die. You were right to question me about Charity. I do have a worry about who would be there for her if I were to…well, you know, if I were to…"

Gwen's mouth went flat. Nathan swallowed around the nervous lump that rose in his throat. This wasn't going the way he'd expected. Not at all.

"You're good with my daughter," he pronounced, making his tone bright and cheery. "And the two of you get along really well."

Was that the beginning of a frown biting into the space between her brows?

"And I think I've been pretty good for Brian. We've, um, developed a real friendship, the two of us have, don't you think?"

Evidently she'd seen the question as rhetorical. With each second that passed it seemed that her facial muscles were growing more taut until her skin looked drawn. She almost looked annoyed. But that was absurd. What possible reason would she have…

Nathan didn't take the time to ponder what he knew to be ridiculous.

"So," he continued, "I was thinking that maybe the two of us might consider…well, don't you think we'd be good…you know…together? For Charity and Brian? And you and me? You know…a family?"

His mouth felt dry as dust. And he realized in that instant that, yes, she definitely did look miffed.

She didn't speak for a long moment. Then her shoulders squared and her brows arched heavenward. "Although your plan sounds quite sensible...I'm not interested."

Gwen stood then, clasping her arms tightly across her chest. "I'll say good-night to you, Nathan. And I'd appreciate it if you lock the door behind you."

She wheeled around and left him sitting there feeling totally bewildered and wondering what in the name of heaven had gone wrong.

"What is it with women? I just don't get it."

As Nathan railed, he paced from one end of his grandfather's kitchen to the other, then turned and looked into Joseph's sleepy, deep-set eyes. The elderly man sat silent, his elbow on the table, his head resting heavily on his palm.

"*She* was the one who argued against my fear of commitment. *She* was the one who said my anxiety over dying prematurely was illogical."

A cool September breeze fluttered the curtains hanging at the window.

"Grandfather, you have to understand. While working in New York, I saw good men die. I watched their families mourn." His jaw set. "That grief was something I didn't want anyone in my life to experience, so I didn't let anyone in my life."

He looked unseeingly around the kitchen. "But Gwen didn't hesitate to dispute my thinking. She made me see that anyone could depart this life by simply stepping out onto the street, but when I went over there tonight to tell her I finally agreed with her, that I've changed my mind, that I thought we should be together—'' he directed his gaze at Joseph ''—she turned me down. Said she wasn't interested.''

Frustration had him throwing up his hands. ''Wasn't she the one who thanked me, over and over, for spending time with Brian? Wasn't she the one who said I was a good role model for the boy? And hasn't she gone out of her way to make a good impression on Charity? Not just as a teacher, but as someone who is truly concerned for my daughter's welfare?'' Disappointment had him shaking his head. ''She loves me. She's said it. Plainly. Why can't she see that our being together—the four of us as a family—makes perfect sense?''

Nathan fell quiet, feeling empty and all questioned out. Gwen's response to his plea was baffling.

Softly Joseph asked, ''That's the reasoning you presented?''

The reply forming on Nathan's tongue went unsaid when the old man emitted a shoulder-shaking chortle. Nathan's knee-jerk reaction was to feel offended, but he ignored it. This man raised him. This man was shrewd, astute, sensible. His grandfather had little in the way of formal education, but his wisdom ran deep.

''First of all,'' his grandfather said, ''both of you are wrong about the end of life on earth. Death is nothing to fear. No life ends until the Spirit Father says it is time. Do you believe a man with a knife is more powerful than the Great One? How can you possibly think that a misguided teen—even with a loaded gun in his hand—is superior to Kit-tan-it-to'wet?'' His mouth became a firm line, then he pronounced, ''Never.''

Joseph pointed his index finger at his beloved grandson. "You think I don't know about that jar of lucky pennies you keep in your office?" He shook his head, his long gray hair swinging gently. "Life and death have nothing whatsoever to do with luck. None of us leaves this world until the Great Spirit says it is time for us to pass into the Other Place. Whether a person believes that or not makes no difference. What is, is."

Every nuance of his grandfather's weariness seemed to have disappeared, replaced with a fierce passion.

"You have been foolish to believe you should go through this life alone simply because you fear your own mortality…and fear the tears and grief of those you would leave behind."

Nathan's head dipped. "You're right, Grandfather. I've been foolish."

"In more ways than one."

Indignant, Nathan stared hard at Joseph. He refrained from commenting, but he couldn't help feeling confused by his grandfather's attack.

Joseph sighed. "When a woman is in love, the last thing she wants to hear is practical logic. Making sense isn't important. Telling Gwen that she and her brother and you and your daughter would make a good family was a mistake. A foolish mistake. Gwen wants to hear that you're besotted with her."

"But I *am* besotted with her!" Nathan was too distraught to realize that before that moment, the word *besotted* hadn't even been in his vocabulary. But it fit how he felt about Gwen. To a T.

"Then go tell her that and let me get back to bed."

Joseph lifted his hand to stifle a yawn as Nathan bolted from the kitchen.

When Nathan's repeated knock on Gwen's front door garnered no response, he should have given up and gone away. Any normal man would have. But he realized this wasn't an ordinary circumstance, so he was damned if he was going yield so easily. He came here to straighten out the muddled mess he'd created, and he meant to do it.

The porch railing was smooth under his fingers as he descended the stairs. The grass muffled his steps as he perused the darkened windows, wondering which one Gwen might be behind.

If the neighbors were to see him skulking around her house in the dark, they might make a call to the police station. Now wouldn't that be something? Him being reported as a peeping Tom?

A bush growing close to the house was perfect cover and he didn't waste any time slipping behind it. His feet crunched on the gravel that had obviously been laid to deter the growth of weeds.

As surreptitiously as possible, he peeked in the window. The shade had been raised about six inches to let in the night breeze, but the filmy sheers blocked his view.

He was just about to turn away when the curtain was shoved aside and a pert little nose and a pair of vivid green eyes appeared close to the screen.

"May I ask what you think you're doing?"

Even angry, her beauty was enough to make his heart *ka-chunk* in his chest. He smiled, but when she glared at him in return, he wrestled it under control.

"I knocked," he told her. "But you didn't answer the door."

"Normally that means that the occupants aren't interested in visitors."

The chill in her tone had his shoulders rounding. Then she relented.

"I wasn't ignoring you, Nathan," she admitted softly. "I didn't hear you at the front door. It was the herd of elephants thrashing around in the bushes that woke me."

Ah, good, she'd made a joke. But she wasn't smiling. Still, he felt compelled to have his say.

"Well, now that you're awake," he said, "can we talk?"

She hesitated only a moment. "I don't think so. I can't see that there's anything more to be said."

"Gwen, please." Feeling the desperate urge to touch her, he reached out. But all he contacted was the fine mesh of the screen. "Please listen to what I have to say."

Gwen stared at him. Then she sighed. "Okay. I'm listening."

A flash of frustration had him frowning. "Can't I come in?"

Her brows rose. "In here? I don't think it's wise."

"Not in your bedroom," he said. "Just...inside."

She pulled back from the window several inches and moonbeams radiated against the white fabric of her nightgown. Her breasts were full and high, their nipples dusky shadows against the material.

Nathan felt himself grow hard at the sight. He knew he should look away, but she was breathtaking.

"Go around to the front door."

She let the curtain drop then, and he actually felt bereft that he was no longer graced with the sight of her.

Wading out of the bush, he made his way to the stoop. The door opened in just a few seconds.

He took in her mass of mussed curls, her milky skin, her sleep-softened eyes, and he wondered how on earth he'd managed to talk himself into living without her all these weeks. Then he remembered how he'd surrendered—more than once—to the passion he felt for her, and he had to admit that his subconscious had known what was best for him all along. He wished he had been smart enough to listen to it.

Instead of offering him entrance as he'd expected, Gwen stepped out onto the front porch and said, "It's a nice night. Let's just talk out here. I don't want to wake Brian again."

"Sure," he said.

She tucked her robe around her as they settled themselves on the top porch step.

Nathan tamped down his case of nerves. He wanted—was *desperate*—to keep his wits about him. To get the words right this time.

"Gwen," he began, "when I was here earlier, I botched things up. I didn't mean any of the things I said—"

He stopped. Tried again. "I meant them, but—"

Again he stopped. "All the things I said before make lots of sense, but those weren't the things—"

Hell, why was this so hard?

His sigh was titanic. He turned to her, gently placed his hands on her forearms.

"I came here earlier to tell you how I feel," he

said. "I came to tell you that I'd changed my mind about our being together."

"Yes," she told him tightly, "I heard all that you—"

"Shh." He placed an index finger gently on her luscious lips. "I love you, Gwen. Do you hear me? I love you."

Something sparked in her green gaze. Was it hope?

Just to be certain there was no misunderstanding this time around, he repeated, "I love you."

The beginning of a smile curled her mouth.

Sensing he was on the correct path now, he rushed down it. "I know that I can't predict the future. And I wouldn't want to. But whether I live to forty or four hundred, I want to spend every single day I've got left here on earth with you. Not for my daughter. Not for your brother. But for me. And for you."

Yes, that really was joyous expectation he read in her eyes, lighting her whole face.

"We belong together, Gwen." He took a moment to study her features. "The love in my heart is so big, I'm afraid it will burst right out of my chest."

Her smile was bright and shining now, and although he knew such a thing could never happen— love couldn't possibly rip open a man's chest—it seemed that the illogical declaration was just what she needed to hear.

"Oh, Nathan," she breathed, "I've waited so long to hear you say that."

He pulled her tightly to him, her scent filling his nostrils, her velvet skin causing his own flesh to prickle with overwhelming need.

"I know you have." His voice was husky as he

inched closer. "And I'm sorry I've been so stubborn." And closer. "So sorry."

Elation burst from her in a light puff of laughter. "But I wouldn't want you any other way! I love you, too."

Nathan kissed her then, their mouths coming together in a meeting that was deliriously hot and sweet. With the taste of her on his tongue, the feel of her in his arms, he knew he'd found the love of his life. Yes, it had taken him a while, but he'd found her just the same.

* * * * *

In December, be sure to look for Grey's story

THE DOCTOR'S PREGNANT PROPOSAL,

as THE THUNDER CLAN series continues...
only from Donna Clayton
and Silhouette Romance!

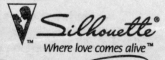

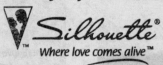

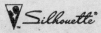

SPECIAL EDITION™

Was it something in the water...
or something in the air?

Because bachelors in Bridgewater, Texas,
are becoming a vanishing breed—fast!

**Don't miss these three exciting stories of Texas
cowboys by favorite author Jodi O'Donnell:**

Deke Larrabie returns to discover
someone *else* he left behind....

THE COME-BACK COWBOY
(Special Edition #1494)
September 2002

Connor Brody meets his match and gives her

THE RANCHER'S PROMISE
(Silhouette Romance #1619)
October 2002

Griff Corbin learns about true
friendship and love when he falls for

HIS BEST FRIEND'S BRIDE
(Silhouette Romance #1625)
November 2002

Available at your favorite retail outlet.

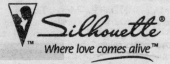

Where love comes alive™

COMING NEXT MONTH